Mercenary Abduction

An Alien Abduction Book

Eve Langlais

Copyright and Disclaimer

Copyright © January 2013, Eve Langlais
Cover Art by Amanda Kelsey © January 2013
Edited by Brandi Buckwine
Copy Edited by Brienna Roberston
Produced in Canada

Published by Eve Langlais
1606 Main Street, PO Box 151
Stittsville, Ontario, Canada, K2S1A3
http://www.EveLanglais.com

ISBN-13: 978-1481958790
ISBN-10: 1481958798

Prologue

〜〜〜〜〜〜〜〜〜〜〜〜〜〜〜〜〜〜〜〜〜〜〜〜〜〜〜

An excerpt from a tattered copy of A Mercenary's Guide to Prosperity.

(Chapter Seven, titled, 'Should I Follow a Religion or God?')

First you need to understand, gods exist. Stop laughing and scoffing, because they do. Some are minor, some major, each featuring differing powers and spheres of influence. Some prefer to stick to one galaxy or solar system, others roam the universe. You'll encounter them during your travels. It's inevitable, however, it is up to the individual mercenary to decide whether he will follow any, and which.

Advantages are possible when you decide to worship a deity such as added strength or invulnerability, but keep in mind, all things come with a price. Involving yourself in the religion of one god may put you at odds with the tenets of another. In some cases, this might mean war, so see Appendix Thirty-nine for a proper listing of rates to charge in case your mercenary services are required for hire.

Returning to the issue of gods – joining a religion, or not, is up to you. Study your options well, though, because once you make your choice, it's usually for life. For a full roster of the various documented deities, please read, *Gods of the Universe* (in alphabetical order) by Sualc Atnas, available universe-wide wherever alcohol, pornography, and weapons of mass destruction are sold. Locations that do not carry copies should be reported so that a member from the mercenary order might show the shop owners the advantage in carrying such a prized manual.

While we highly recommend the purchase of the guide to *Gods of The Universe* (available in electronic download, subliminal feed, a pallet of stone tablets, and even outlawed printed paper), we feel it important to note the existence of one god in particular, a deity who bears the most watching. He goes by many names; Llokii, Puuka, Murphy, among others. A more pesky character you'll never meet.

While this particular god seems to ascribe to male characteristics, he belongs to no known race. As a matter of fact, no one can agree on his natural form as he seems capable of changing it at will, a shape-shifter who can wear any guise and appear in numerous places at once. He does not seem to strive for power or domination, nor does he seem to crave wealth. Is he good or evil? Again, he doesn't seem to really care, although, he does seem to find humor sometimes in his antics.

Murphy's esoteric strength is difficult to gauge, for while he doesn't physically destroy, he can topple empires sometimes with a single meaningless act or word. He seems to exist nowhere, and yet his influence can crop up anywhere. I've heard many swear even our innermost thoughts are not secure.

Phantom or actual being? It depends on who you ask and what you believe, but all agree he is cunning. Unpredictable. Vain. Powerful. Subtle.

Blatant. Most of all, though, he is never to be underestimated.

To the few he befriends, he is an invaluable asset and ally. To those who've done him ill…expect the unexpected, for Murphy follows one rule, one tenet, one law above all, and it can be summed up simply: if it can go wrong, it will.

To avoid him, never, ever, not for a single moment, ever say aloud, or even think you have everything thought out. Never brag you have the perfect plan or a foolproof idea. Cockiness will draw his attention and then…you better hope you have a Plan B, but prepare for Plan C or D, because with Murphy, you can never predict a sure outcome.

But we can guarantee one thing. If he's set his sights on you, then you are most assuredly frukxed!

Chapter One

〰〰〰〰〰〰〰〰〰〰〰〰〰〰〰〰〰〰〰〰〰〰〰

In the obsidian galaxy, far, far away…

The holographic monocle over his eye zoomed in on his target. Lying flat on his stomach atop a gently sloped, slightly gritty, surfaced roof, Makl kept his movements to a minimum. Given the various notices prohibiting anyone but those with valid work permits access to his location, he did his best to remain out of sight, not an easy task for a warrior who preferred the limelight. For several galactic units now he'd ignored the rumble in his stomach, the itch in his side, and the one frukxing rock digging into his thigh. He tuned out all the discomforts and distractions a boring stakeout tempted a male with. Nevertheless, a need for surreptitiousness or not, he knew better than to ignore his Aunt Muna's transmission, the insistent buzzing persistent in his ear.

"Auntie, to what do I owe the pleasure?" he purred, even as he meticulously noted the placement and rotation of cameras outside the establishment he cased. Also documented in his notes was how many guards patrolled and at what intervals.

"I trust you're being a good soldier and bringing the family honor?" Aunt Muna didn't waste time on trivialities such as "Hello," and, "How are you?"

"Following in the footsteps of the great ones," he answered as he jotted his findings into his holographic notebook. It and the tool over his eye were some of the best technology he'd ever come across – and stolen.

"In other words, you're fornicating, thieving, and murdering."

He couldn't help but smile at her blunt summary. "As often as I can."

"Excellent. Keep up the good work. Your mother would have been so proud. If you could, though, in between causing havoc and mayhem, I need you to perform an errand for me."

"I'm kind of busy at the moment." Busy planning out his next move and investigating his target, a heist destined to put him at the top of a few wanted lists. He couldn't wait to see the headshots he'd had professionally taken – by none other than the renowned photographer, Notromus – plastered on wanted posters. After weeks of work with the famed artist, they'd finally come up with a portfolio to be proud of. It took time and skill to achieve just the right look of menace mixed with insouciance. Nothing like projecting the right image when carving his name in to history.

"You're too busy?" Uh oh. Makl recognized his aunt's tone. It didn't bode well. "I'm sorry, did you hear me say you had a choice, or would you prefer I tell Tren you were too occupied to help out family?" Said so sweetly. Too softly.

Big uh oh. Makl swallowed hard. "Maybe I spoke too hastily. Did I hear you say this involves Tren?" Family or not, no one wanted to rile that particular male. Makl's older cousin tended to kill first and not care after. Tren – a legend in their family – said questions were for the uncertain. Mercenary rule number thirteen.

Aunt Muna cleared her throat. "Tren is caught up in some important affairs currently or he'd take care of this himself. I think it's a great honor he's willing to trust you with this task."

The high and mighty, infamous former mercenary, now turned cutthroat politician, needed his help? Makl's chest expanded several units. "Of course I'm available to aid him. Family comes first."

"Excellent answer."

"So what am I required for?" Assassination? Kidnapping? Hostage situation? Ooh, hopefully an extremely difficult acquisition of a top-secret scientific breakthrough. Makl loved a challenge, and the gadgets such endeavors brought.

"It's a highly sensitive mission of utmost importance."

Makl paused in his note-taking, intrigued.

"Possibly dangerous."

Sounded promising.

"It's not something we can ask of anyone else."

Better and better. Makl almost held his breath as he waited for her to get to the point.

"We need you to fetch a nanny."

Removing his earpiece, Makl blew on it, rubbed it on his shirt, wiggled a finger in his ear, then returned the hearing unit to his ear. "Excuse me, Auntie? I think I must have misunderstood. Could you repeat the mission?"

"You need to fetch us a nanny."

He took a moment to process her words, looking for a hidden meaning. He came up with nothing. "Nanny, as in someone who cares for an infant?"

"Of course. Do you know of any other type?" His aunt's exasperation came through loud and clear.

Well, excuse him, but the mission still made no sense. "Why would you need me to hire a nanny? I have no bastards." At least none that he was aware of.

"Not for you, idiot. For Tren."

"He was careless enough to leave bastards behind? I'll bet his mate isn't happy about that." He'd met Megan, the shrill human who was insane enough to marry his cousin, and had to admit he didn't see the attraction to the pale-skinned barbarian. Not that he'd mention that to his cousin's face, not if he wanted to live.

"We don't need a nanny for anyone's bastards. The position is for his heir who has the mightiest lungs and temper I've ever seen. He'll be the greatest warrior ever when he grows up." Aunt Muna practically gushed and Makl bit back a growl.

I will be the greatest warrior, once I get my name and face out there. His determination to succeed might have made him a little more brash than usual with his aunt, that and the several star systems separating them. "You want me to drop everything to fetch a nanny for Tren's whelp? Are you still in possession of your faculties, Auntie? Do I need to speak to my uncle about putting you on some medication?" He regretted his blithe answer as soon as it left his lips.

"Do you need me to show you how not to talk back to your elders?" she replied sweetly. "Again."

No. Not again. Once was enough, thank you. He never did manage to rid himself of the scars from the last time she taught him some manners. Aunt Muna took her role as female guardian after his mother died very seriously. When she spoke, everyone ran. It kept them in shape.

He gave in, just not gracefully. "So what am I looking for? Something with lots of arms, no sense of smell, and more patience than is normal?"

"We tried that. We got an eight-armed Gunilian hummer. She went hoarse. The five-armed and deaf Answuya ran off in tears. We need something more drastic than that, which is why we require your services. You have to fetch us a human nanny."

A human? As in forbidden by some powerful entities, living on the other side of the frukxing universe, barbarian status human? By the stars, how fascinating. And dangerous. "Humans are off limits. You know it's punishable by death to get caught pirating them."

"Are you afraid of a measly sentence like that? You know Tren had over six thousand crimes stacked against him by the time he retired. It took forever to clear the paperwork on them once he ascended to his position on the galactic council."

Way to throw Tren's daunting success in his face. Makl still worked on his first thousand. Make that first five hundred. Apparently, some of his kills weren't flamboyant enough to merit attention. "You want a human, I'll get you a human. What's the payment?"

"My thanks."

She expected him to work for free? He gnashed his sharpened teeth. "A generous gift. And from Tren?"

Aunt Muna snorted.

Yeah, Tren would never frukxing thank him, not with words or credits. It just wasn't his way, but he might hold off killing him if Makl accidentally got on his bad side – which he tended to inadvertently do quite often. *Looks like I'm going to fetch a barbarian.* As if Makl possessed a choice. Free job or not, he'd do what his aunt asked because he liked – and feared – her.

He sighed. "How soon do you need it?"

"You mean her? Yesterday."

"Anything else I need to know? Qualities I should look for?"

"How the frukx should I know? Just find us a human female to care for the child. Megan's doing her best, but she's only one person and this child is demon possessed, bless his mighty heart."

Makl made one last ditch effort to avoid the task. "You do realize I'm nowhere near that galaxy."

"Then you better get moving. This errand is of utmost importance." Aunt Muna shouted the last bit over the strident screams of a baby. Ripping the earpiece from his head, Makl winced as the howl bounced around inside his skull. Good lungs indeed.

Pocketing his earpiece, he turned his attention back to the building he'd studied over the course of the last few days. He was finished here now. No point in observing it any further, not when he'd have to return at a later time to finish the job. And all because of a stupid errand – a free, no glory, no credits errand – he couldn't refuse.

Pocketing his tools, he climbed down from the building he'd scaled, people not daring to say a word despite him obviously being up to no good. Cowards. What did a miscreant have to do in order to get noticed? With a snarl on his lips, he made his way to street level and grumbled under his breath as he stalked through the marketplace.

Sent on an errand indeed. Did his Aunt Muna not realize he had more important things to do than to fetch a nanny for his stupid cousin? He was meant to do great things. Dastardly deeds, not act the part of errand boy. What was so hard about placing an ad and conducting interviews until someone could be found to care for the spawn created by his egotistical cousin Tren and his barbarian female? Next thing he knew, they'd ask him to buy toys, or mind the child. How degrading.

Tren should find his own human. He'd already accidentally abducted one, his mate, Megan. How hard could it be for him to mistakenly kidnap a second?

Although, the idea of flouting the laws and brazenly going to the barbarian planet to steal a female did sound like fun. Earth was considered off limits, not that everyone obeyed that particular edict. Disregarding the strictly enforced law might get him some recognition if word got around.

While his reputation as a fighter was building, Makl still had a ways to go before he came out from under the shadow of his numerous cousins. The frukxing jerks. The problem with being born in an illustrious family known for its misdeeds universe-wide was standing out. Everything he did had already been done before, and in many cases more flamboyantly – as family and officials liked to remind him.

But not for long. Soon I'll do something so crazy, so clever, they won't have a choice but to see what a mighty mercenary I am. Even if he had to go on a murderous rampage to achieve it.

The bazaar was in full swing as he blended back into the crowd. Clad in a shadowy grey cape that swirled around his frame, the tip of it reaching the tops of his boots, he glared at those in his path. Most moved out of his way. Those that didn't? He wisely left the bigger, meaner looking ones alone. Tough and seeking to make a name for himself didn't mean Makl engaged in stupid battles –unless someone offered him the right price. Mercenary rule number one: don't fight unless you're getting paid. If it didn't give you credits, then why waste the effort and chance of an injury? Of course, exceptions to the rule existed. Rule number eight stated no tolerance for insults or slurs. While number fifteen, which he personally felt should have been a sub-clause to number eight, advocated revenge at all cost.

Some might mock the rules of mercenary living, but Makl studied them religiously, memorizing his handbook – *A Mercenary's Guide to Prosperity.* Creased and worn, the mercenary rule book was a present from his father who'd seen how Makl idolized Tren. What male didn't? As a child and a teen, he'd hear about the exploits of his great cousin. The big and mean male brought massive amounts of honor and riches to their house, but what Makl truly coveted was the shining adulation in everyone's eyes whenever his deeds were recounted.

Makl wanted that glory, to bring that smile of pride to his family's face. It was why he worked so hard to achieve evil success and why he lived by the mercenary rules. With the mantras he lived by guiding his steps and his fortune, he gained notoriety. He also still lived to fight another day and his credit account grew. Now if only he could achieve a big score. Something to really make him the number-one-wanted-male in the universe.

He'd hoped to accomplish that here. And he still would, just not today, apparently. Stupid frukxing family.

Grumbling some more, Makl headed toward his favorite brothel, determined to relieve his cock before undertaking the stupidly long voyage to the planet Earth. Rule number five – keep your cock exercised lest lust cloud your judgment. Makl took this dictum very seriously, most males he knew did. Prone to long space voyages, often alone or with a handful of other males, all good mercenaries spent a good chunk of time and their fortune when docked emptying their cocks. Each time Makl came, he could swear he felt himself getting more clear-headed and smarter, so was it any wonder he never neglected this part of his training?

Intent on attaining that state of *clarity,* he did his best to ignore the booths of wares. Not an easy task. Tasseled and painted with bright colors, displaying riches and rarities from around the universe, everything served to distract – and tempted his twitching fingers. Spices, their aromas lifting the mood in some cases, dulling the spirit in others.

Gems and jewelry, some with boulder-sized stones to please even the most avarice minded of mistresses, gleamed. Stalls with displays of fabric so bright it hurt the eyes, in more colors than the universe intended, were hard to view without the protection of glasses. But it was the noise that was the worst. Everything seemed to pile together to create an unpleasant rumble of sound. Even some of the delicate finery added to the cacophony. How, you ask? In the Obsidian galaxy, legal or not, you could find actual living, breathing skeins of silk. You heard that right. Living fabric existed, very rare, forbidden, and expensive, but ridiculously comfortable, or so he'd heard. At least the tissue stopped screaming once the seamstresses finished their stitching and cutting the illegal stuff into a garment. Although, Makl had heard the occasional whimper when he removed a more delicate piece with his teeth.

But he digressed. Not a good idea amidst the madness of the market where the hundreds of voices begged listening, movement bore watching, and danger possibly sneaked up on him. He hoped. In a place like this, there were always predators looking to make victims of the newcomers. The weak.

Makl didn't fall into that category. Strong as any alien present – for his weight class – he didn't doubt his ability to prevail. Although, keeping his hunger in check? His belly rumbled at the smells… Mmm, the temptation to gorge himself almost slowed his steps. Food abounded all around, freshly made and enhanced to tempt every palette. Some were upfront kiosks, hawking their steaming or smoking dishes. In some cases, the decadent aromas sifted out from restaurants in the tightly packed buildings where one took the chance of becoming part of the menu. No one ever starved in the marketplace where every *hunger* could be fed, legal or not.

In the center of all the aisles of chaos, winding streets intentionally built to funnel traffic, an open area existed, but was crowded at the moment. An auction was obviously in progress, which meant no getting across quickly to the other side. Stupid design. Either he waited it out, or he had to back track and take a more circuitous path, which would totally cut into his fornicating time.

Not for the first time, Makl wished he'd not gotten booted from the Hairy Dual Cleft on this side of the plaza. Alas, combining his business – the messy kill of a space captain whose wife caught him cheating – and his pleasure – a lovely gal he should have probably paid in retrospect – meant he now had to travel a little farther to ease his sexual needs.

An unmarried male had two choices in the cities he visited: take his chances with a female fighter, or find a whore. Females of the races most compatible to his kind were for some reason always scarcer than the males. Odd, but true, unless you counted the Zonian planet where a violent female class held sway. But no sane male ever went there expecting to leave alive.

Too many beings with cocks meant laws existed to protect the females, from strangers at least. Single women were not to be bothered under penalty of death. Fathers took their role as chaperone seriously, but the mothers were fanatic. Virginity went for a high price, and seeing as how there were always males seeking mates to birth their own sons, a family could make a pretty penny with the right marriage or sale.

Only a stupid warrior messed with a prized virgin. Makl didn't need to rub his posterior to remember the errors of his way. So whores it was, seeing as how the female fighters he'd encountered could often pass for men – *shudder*. And since the Hairy Dual Cleft fiasco, Makl even remembered to pay his sexual partners and tip them – with credits instead of just orgasms.

As he stood on the edge of the crowd, debating whether to wait or skirt the disturbance, he finally took note of the sight on stage.

"I'll be frukxed," he muttered.

It seemed the minor goddess of Karma – from the lost galaxy no one could remember – was smiling his way because standing on the raised dais, dressed in a floor-length cloak, head bowed, hands clasped, was a human, or so the announcer claimed as he extolled her many virtues. What a long list of attributes – trained dancer, accomplished chef, a player of nine instruments – the demure human came with a certificate vouching for her maidenhead, which would make her fetch a hefty price.

Not that Makl planned to pay for her.

As the Galactic Avenger, he would take her from right under her new owner's nose. And maybe laugh while he did it. He didn't think Tren or Jaro ever did that. Tren usually glowered. Jaro gave people a toothy grin. Makl would chuckle menacingly. Or should he just smile coldly? He really needed to decide on his look so people would have something to talk about when they recounted his daring deeds.

But he got ahead of himself. First, he needed to acquire a certain human.

Settling on an expression of bored disinterest, he skulked on the edge of the crowd, noting who seemed most intent on bidding, sizing up the competition. It vaguely occurred to him that his Aunt Muna probably wouldn't approve of him hiring a virgin trained in the finest of the erotic arts, but then again, she didn't give him exactly much of a list. *Besides, surely a female trained to deal with difficult men should have no problem handling a baby.*

And it would save him the cost of a trip to the outer reaches…

If the whole virgin thing was a problem, Makl knew of a way to get rid of it. And save hard earned credits in the process.

Could his luck get any better?

It could. Makl's exhale of breath halted as the female on stage lifted her head, the delicate draping of cloth over her hair framing a perfectly oval face. Sporting two eyes, one nose and a set of lips like him but in a pinkish hue, she was enchanting. Pure. Perfect. Her skin…ooh her skin gleamed a pale, icy white. It contrasted nicely with her dark, delicately arched brows and her full, kissable lips. How easy to imagine her flesh as a light foil for his dark purple tone. The thought was enough to make his cock stir.

Yet, her delicate beauty wasn't the only thing that drew him. Eyes of velvety chocolate – a decadent sweet treat he'd stumbled across a time or two– big and startled, stared at him, and he ogled her right back. Maybe this whole nanny thing wouldn't end up such a chore after all. By abducting the human on stage, he would shave days off his schedule. He could even take his time, to save fuel of course, and add several galactic revolutions to his trip back to Aunt Muna's. Plenty of time to deflower the virgin and ruin her for all other males. Megan would probably thank him.

I'll be a frukxing hero. In more ways than one.

Chapter Two

〜〜〜〜〜〜〜〜〜〜〜〜〜〜〜〜〜〜〜〜〜〜〜〜〜〜〜

Olivia fluttered her lashes, keeping them demurely downcast lest the men in the crowd – and the things with too many arms, eyes, and appendages she'd prefer not dwell on – think her too forward. It was important to her benefactor that she appear well behaved, gentle, and soft spoken. The perfect female. Fetch the highest price possible; that was the plan. She'd not spent all her time training, then getting groomed – plucked, shaved, skin sanded and moisturized by too many tentacles on the beautician to count – to not succeed. She just hoped she earned a high price.

She, make that they, had worked hard to get her here, the infamous Obsidian Galaxy marketplace, a place avoided by all but the bravest—stupidest— and richest. A lawless world ruled by thieves and murderers, whose warped idea of honor changed from day to day, where anything could be bought and sold, killed or appropriated. A place where sin didn't exist, only the right price. The perfect place to auction a forbidden barbarian human, like herself, to a crowd of the wealthiest – most debauched – beings in the universe.

The dozens of greedy – and lust filled – glances trained on her made her skin crawl worse than the bath she'd suffered with the suzzule worms. Nasty little critters, they chomped off the dead layers of cells, giving her skin a fresh, dewy appearance. She rather thought she looked like a pale ghost after the disgusting experience, but the specialist in charge of presentation claimed it was all the rage. Personally, she considered it a waste of time and money, because other than a few, tastefully done images, they dressed her in a gown from ankle to neck, which they then covered with a voluminous cloak of pure white. Spun from a feathery light fabric, it covered her from head to toe, hiding her shape from view while affording a glimpse of her tall, slender frame. It seemed surprise over blatant display tended to enflame rather than detract from appetites, not all of them the lusty variety. She could practically imagine some of the odder-looking specimens in the crowd hefting forks and knives in their sweaty palms – and suckered tentacles.

Bloody freaking aliens. Years in space still hadn't gotten her used to the various forms life took. Forget the cute E.T.s and green Martians she vaguely recalled from the shows she watched growing up – the reality was the universe held a lot of butt ugly creatures, most of which oozed fluids she preferred not to think about or smelled funny.

The focus of attention from so many strangers, Olivia couldn't stem her unease. Too many things could happen. Oh God, the things that could go wrong. She knew the laws of chance – she'd learned them firsthand. Expect the unexpected.

Not today, please. Let Murphy and his games stay away.

Inhaling, she took an unsteady breath and let it out in a tremulous rush. A few E.T.s in the front of the crowd caught the nervous gesture and the number scrolling on the screens ringing the arena area flashed in red neon. Ten million. Twenty…

The amount of credits strangers would pay for a certified virgin, a human virgin – barbarian and forbidden – boggled her mind. By the end of today, one of the creatures bidding in front of her would own her, could do as he liked with her, good or ill, but only once they paid up and signed the contract.

The earpiece in her ear crackled to life and orders came through. "Give them something to whet their appetite. Show them a little fear."

Not hard. Olivia wrung her hands, the long sleeves of her robe not completely hiding her pale, slim fingers. She didn't have to fake the tremor. The numbers kept scrolling steadily upward. She lifted her gaze and bit her lower lip as she scanned the audience, not letting her glance stay on any one alien too long. The variety of life in the room staggered her. What would a Pkl – an aquatic race with no actual corporeal form unless a puddle counted – do with her?

It seemed more than a fair share of races gathered to watch and bid. Tusked, tall, short, fat, and thin, in the Obsidian Galaxy, most especially the black market on the planet That-Didn't-Exist, races came together and respected the rules of this pirate world or paid the consequences. Apparently, there were some punishments worse than death. One of them screamed out the quarter galactic minutes for those who forgot their timepieces.

Unable to tell who battled hardest to win her, she meant to return her stare to the floor when an amused set of ice blue, almost clear eyes caught hers.

Her first thought was, *What's a handsome fellow doing in a place like this to purchase flesh?*

Sporting dark mauve skin, a straight nose, a chin with the hint of a dimple, and shockingly white hair that hung to his shoulders in waves, she couldn't deny the E.T.'s handsome features. So what craven secret did he hide? Or was he simply here as a guard? Wearing a silvery cloak, she could see no emblem on his chest, nor tell for that matter how far his normalcy extended. From the neck up, he appeared more or less like her, if purple. From the neck down, he could have eight legs and a hairy belly.

Who cared? Despite the fact he kept that amused lilt to his lips as they continued to lock gazes, she didn't get the impression he'd come to bid. She wasted time exchanging glances with him, and it wouldn't do to make the others in the crowd mad, or lose interest. She peeked away, and yet her skin tickled, knowing he still watched. Of course he did, she was the focal point of this whole bloody affair.

She fidgeted, found her head moving in the purple guy's direction, and stopped it. Why the curiosity? She didn't really care what he did here. Either he bid or he didn't. Either she'd imagined his interest or not. Did he still stare? Her gut said yes. But how to know unless she looked?

Without volition, she peeked in his direction. Intuition wrong. He no longer stood there, yet her skin tingled as if he still watched. As if under someone else's control, her eyes slid to the left and there he was, standing almost at the head of the crowd, the hood of his cloak pulled up, but she could see his eyes, those clear, expressive orbs. His black lips curved in a grin, which widened when he realized she'd caught him. He winked.

She almost tossed her head, but didn't want to give him the satisfaction of knowing he unsettled her. She broke eye contact, but checked him out in his new angle. His cloak ended mid-calf and she spotted a pair of black boots—only two feet, how rare—the leather scuffed but clean. She couldn't judge his height, but pegged him at least as tall as her, maybe a touch taller. Most interesting of all? He didn't hold an auction box. No transmitter with a small view screen for bidding, which meant he wasn't a client. *And not worthy of my attention.*

A voice whispered in her ear. "What's got you distracted? Don't say anything. Just stick to what I told you. Eyes down. Hands clasped. It's almost over. And a mighty fine catch, too."

But Olivia missed the final bid, because with another naughty wink, the purple stranger melted into the crowd, disappearing almost magically from sight. Yet, she couldn't help a sense of unease at the last playful glance, almost as if he promised to return. Impossible. Once she went to her new owner, she'd never see him again. She'd hopefully never see anyone from this crowd again.

She put the stranger from her mind and focused on the task at hand. Auction over, she took mincing steps off the stage, leaving to prepare herself for the change of ownership.

Staff surrounded her as soon as she hit the preparation area, the hum of their voices only partially penetrated.

"Never seen such a high price…"

"Do you think he plans to eat her?"

"Lucky slave. Her new owner is filthy rich. She'll live like a queen."

If queens were sluts. Idiots. No matter how long she lived among aliens, she remembered enough of her old life on earth to know women weren't treated with the same rights out here in the vast galaxy than back home on earth. *And they call us the barbarians.* Advanced technology, ability to travel the stars or not, Olivia thought the universe had a lot to learn about equality of the sexes. It baffled her that males would pay just about anything for the prize between a woman's thighs. Then again, who was she to judge the greedy aliens so harshly? It was her own mother who sold her to this life in the first place. Now there was a memory she wished she could forget.

Shoved into a chair, she let the beautician and stylists fuss over her. They tweaked her hair, touched up her coloring, toning it down from its current enhanced state meant for the bright lights of the stage to something more suited to an intimate setting. Perfume enveloped her in a scented cloud and her nose wiggled.

"Don't you dare sneeze," the voice in her earpiece warned, a spectacular feat given the speaker wasn't even in the same room.

"How do you do that?" She spoke aloud, the staff used to her one-sided conversations with her benefactor.

"I'm always watching."

"You know that's creepy rather than reassuring."

The familiar chuckle made her roll her eyes, earning her a pinch from the artist recoating her lashes.

"So, are you clear on the next step?"

Olivia held in a sigh. "We only practiced it a million times. I can handle it. It's what you groomed me for."

"Don't let me down."

"I won't." She hoped.

The connection went dead and Olivia sagged. A seeming lifetime of lessons all boiled down to this moment, the moment that would change the course of her future.

Odd how that thought should make her think of ice blue eyes.

*

Makl turned off his cape's cloaking ability, a rare and expensive piece of technology he'd borrowed – more or less. It wasn't like its previous owner had need of it – anymore. Not his fault the fellow had a big mouth, one he couldn't help but run after Makl treated him to some extra strong Quergon ale. A braggart should know how to hold his liquor, even the laced kind.

It seemed a shame to let the luxurious cloak go to waste when the owner met the sharp end of a dagger – his, of course – especially since the cloak of invisibility was one of only two of its kind. Or so Makl discovered from the inventor when he tracked him down. The maker held the secret of their creation in his head. A brilliant scientist, the cloak maker used his almost magical ability with nanotechnology to escape the prison a very rich patron kept him in – with a little help from Makl.

Then the jerk ran off before Makl could get him to spill the secret of how to make more. He really had to stop being so nice. From now on, manacles stayed on, urge to pee or not.

Ooh, he should totally get some cuffs for the human. And not just to keep her behaved. The things Makl could do to her while she was at his mercy...

First though, he needed to get his hands on her. During the auction, he'd quickly calculated the odds in stealing her from under everyone's nose, but deemed it much too dangerous. A shame. A public feat like that would have made the news for sure – but left him a corpse. Preferring to keep his carcass intact, he instead made plans for after. Once the new owner paid for and received his prize, Makl intended to steal her before said prize got sullied. A traumatized human wouldn't do him any good, but one rescued in the nick of time would prove ever so grateful to the male who saved her. The very handsome, suave, and dare he say dashing hero of the day. Conqueror of the stars. Lover of...

Yeah, he really needed to work on his catch line. Damn his cousins for already stealing the best slogans. It wasn't easy to make his mark and cast his own light upon the shadows left by his illustrious family. Tren, greatest assassin the galaxy ever knew – until now. Jaro, the scourge of the universe –who one day would pale in comparison to Makl – whose reputation got further enhanced when he somehow tamed a fierce Zonian female. Yeah, Makl wasn't sure how to best that feat yet. Most sexual partners fiercer than a Zonian involved damage to male parts. Maybe he'd let Jaro keep that distinction. That still left Brax and Xarn, the bumbling idiots who nobody wanted to become.

Still, even if he only counted Tren and Jaro, with those kinds of reputations preceding him, Makl had to work twice as hard to get noticed. Hence, his visit to the Obsidian Galaxy. Priding itself on having the tightest security, the most decadent pirate pleasures and deals, the challenge to best this den of iniquity just about screamed his name.

If I can steal something valuable, something big, say, like an actual slave, and make it out of here alive? Ha, even his cousins never achieved something so dangerous – *and stupid*, whispered a voice in his head. What the frukx? Since when did he doubt himself?

You're right. Don't bother with doubt. Just do it. It should be fun to watch.

His conscience chose an odd time to speak to him. As if Makl would start listening. *Shut up, conscience, I'll do as I please with no help from you. I've got the goddess Karma on my side.*

That useless female?

Makl's mind seemed flabbergasted. Odd. He knew Karma wouldn't let him down. Not like other wannabe gods he'd heard of.

Arrogant little... For a moment, Makl wondered at his sanity as his mind seemed about to lose its temper – at him! Instantly, his inner psyche quieted. *Angry? No, but disappointed. You've already found a human. How much harder to keep with the first plan as well? Cause twice the havoc.* Pure insanity. Stealing a slave was dangerous enough, but to also go through with his original heist?

Once the idea took hold, it consumed him. Why not make his move even bolder? It would only take a little extra tweaking.

It wasn't as if he didn't already have it all planned out. He'd cased the jewelry boutique – which saw clients by appointment only – in the second quadrant. He knew the priceless bauble he would take – a one of a kind solar diamond with the encased black hole. He'd discerned where the owner stashed it and how he kept it secure. Just not secure enough from Makl and his nimble fingers.

I could do this. The glory of it if he pulled it off… He could almost see the headlines. The recognition.

He'd thought he'd have to forget his original devious deed when Aunt Muna called and told him to bring back a human nanny. Travel to that barbarian system and kidnap a human? Sure it was against the law and hardcore, but so done already. By his cousin Tren, as a matter of fact.

Why waste the fuel when, lo and behold, he found just what his aunt ordered. A human girl. Did he care about her credentials? She was female. Females tended children. Wasn't it like a natural instinct, like knowing how to please a male?

Finding a human with such a high price tag? If he could both kidnap her and take the diamond, why he'd end up infamous. Makl, the mighty thief. Hmmm, that made him sound paltry. Perhaps Makl the invincible.

Or Makl the arrogant. Stop dithering around and get moving already. The auction is over. Credits now changed banks. Goods were being transferred. Time to spring into action and pray Karma was watching.

Forget that petty goddess. You've got me. The new voice in his head should have worried Makl. Okay, it did a little, but maybe his newfound madness would finally allow him to achieve the greatness he always wanted.

Or a permanent hole in his chest.

Chapter Three

Olivia listened with half an ear as her worried benefactor whispered last minute instructions via her embedded communicator.

"Don't look him in the eye. Any of them. They take it as a sign of aggression and will turn you into stone, which is painful to get reversed. Watch the left tentacles, they have a numbing agent in the tips."

"What's in the ones on the right?"

"Lips."

Olivia shuddered. "So it eats with its finger things?"

"No, those are just for licking and sipping. Its actual mouth is in its chest. Ringed in razor sharp teeth. You shouldn't go near it."

"Stay away from teeth. Check. Anything else I should know?"

"Nope, that about sums it up. You did good. Just remember what I told you and all will be fine."

Olivia wished she shared that optimism, and yet, a nagging sense wouldn't let her relax. She'd learned to trust her gut over the years. It never steered her wrong and it told her, screamed at her as a matter of fact, to watch out. Maybe she imagined it, but she could almost touch the sensation of something big in the air. Change was coming. She knew it with a certainty she'd only felt a few times before in her life. Hopefully, the change wouldn't prove detrimental to her health.

Veiled and ready for seduction, Olivia kept pace with the guards sent by her new owner. A ring of creatures wearing bulletproof armor and towering over her by a good foot or more, she couldn't see a thing around her, but people sure could hear them coming. *Clomp. Clomp. Clomp.*

The monotony of the steps lulled her so when they suddenly stopped, she stumbled into the back of a guard.

"Oops. Sorry there, big guy." She smiled apologetically, not that he budged. Tough crowd.

Someone spoke in a hushed whisper and she heard the sound of a door sliding open, the mechanic whoosh distinctive. The ring of guards around her parted, leaving her an opening. With small, measured steps, she stepped through and entered decadence. Her slippered feet sank into a plush carpet. Muted light eased the eyes. The strains of a popular galactic melody piped through the air along with the calming scent of hoha leaves – part muscle relaxer, part aphrodisiac. It was rare, thus expensive, and her new owner burned it. Wealth at its finest.

Her wealth, soon. Once the transaction was complete, this type of decadence would belong to her. Awesome.

Head bowed, she headed to the desk in the room behind which sat her new owner. Ugly fellow. Gray warty skin, wisps of yellow hair tufting from the oddest places, and a distracting amount of red-veined, bulbous eyes. He wore a loose robe from which projected at least six waving tentacles. She noted their length and kept well out of reach.

A pair of guards stood behind the guy who paid such a high price for her, appearing every bit as grim and menacing as the ones who brought her. *But big doesn't mean better.* The best fighter she knew lacked in size, but when it came to incapacitating larger foes, she'd never seen anything more awe-inspiring. What a shame she'd never managed to achieve that kind of skill. But Olivia excelled in other areas.

Coming to a standstill before the massive desk carved from wood, similar to what she recalled from her years on earth, she waited for orders like a good little slave.

"Lift your veil." The command was spoken in a dulcet tone, a neat translation feat accomplished by the transmitter buried in her ear canal. It also provided auditory protection lest the alien being's unusually high decibel level explode her eardrums. She'd seen it happen once. Not pretty.

Hands shaking slightly, she took her time folding back the lacy headdress draping her head, revealing her face bit by bit, every inch the innocent maiden. It seemed those hours of practice paid off. A satisfied grunt left the tentacled male. He waved his appendages around. "Come closer that I might touch your skin and ensure it is not a mask."

Touch before the deal was done? Her teacher warned her about that. She shook her head and tsked. "Your scanners would have detected weapons or glamour upon my entry. We both know what you see is what you get." She tempered her rebuke with a smile.

What she assumed was a chuckle shook the bulbous body. "A little bit of spirit. I like it. The goods seem to be as promised. Transfer the funds."

Her new owner tilted the screen and let her watch as a large sum of credits moved from his account into another. A message flashed up with the code word she'd memorized to let her know all was good.

The creature in front of her now owned her. *Until he sells me – or death do us part.*

Some of her tension eased. Olivia smiled. "Master."

"Take off your clothes."

Abrupt fellow. She lifted her gaze and flicked a glance at the two guards. "But we are not alone, my lord."

"My guards go where I go."

"My master is generous then."

Her words took him by surprise. "Generous? Who told you such nonsense?"

"Why no one, my mighty lord. I just assumed it given you would share your first encounter with me, a moment I've waited for in seclusion my whole life, a pleasure you paid so dearly for. Who else but a generous male like yourself would share this most unique of moments, even if only visually. Who else but the most charitable of masters would let others indulge in the glory we shall achieve together as you show me your supreme prowess?"

At least half of the alien's eyes glazed over while the other half narrowed shrewdly. Had she said too much? "You're right. I did pay a fortune. How can I brag about your rarity if others are aware of it? Guards. Leave us."

The right one leaned down to whisper something, probably something along the lines of "Are you nuts?" Bad move. The wealthy and powerful never liked it when their minions told them what to do, even if for their own good. This one proved no different. Males always suffered the same arrogance no matter their shape or place in the galaxy. Her new master's mien darkened to an ominous green. "You think this mere unarmed slip of a girl can harm me? Do you take me for a weakling?"

No, but she did hope he owned enough testosterone to let her taunt make him do something foolish, say, like send his guards away. She really didn't want anyone to see what happened next. Her stomach churned as it was. She didn't need an audience.

Remember the lessons. Easy to remind herself, but now faced with her hardest task ever, she hoped she could pull it off. Failure wasn't an option. Taking a deep breath, she waited to see what would happen next.

*

Makl wanted to applaud how well the human virgin dealt with the alien who bought her. Wanted to congratulate her with the awesomeness of his person, but didn't lest he give his position away. He'd wondered how he'd take out both guards, subdue the rich alien, and muffle the girl so that no one heard or suspected a thing until he'd vanished into thin air. Lucky him, the slave took care of the problem for him. With the guards gone, he only really needed to worry about the big alien waiting to get it on with Makl's human virgin.

My virgin. Yeah, he'd already imagined her deflowering countless times once he got into position, blending into the room's drapes through the use of his cloak, standing still lest he ruin the illusion. It wasn't easy, especially since his fantasies involving the pale-skinned barbarian had her always thanking him in carnal ways. By the stars, the number of times he'd mentally debauched her, had her scream his name, sob it, rake his back... *Maybe I should aim for the universe's greatest lover?* Damn his subconscious for snickering.

I'm getting ahead of the game again. First, I need to save the girl.

As easy as frukxing a whore on the flowery planet of Druella – a world few ever left once they inhaled its narcotic and sexual effect. In germination season, the very air dripped with pheromones. Great for ailing sexual appetites, if you didn't mind what you frukxed. Makl, however, drew the line at things with bigger cocks than his. For now, though, he needed to forget Druella. The time to act approached.

The guards, not happy with their orders, stomped out. The door slid shut. The human female spun and surely she did not mean to smile so brightly at the male who'd bought her and made her his sexual slave for life?

"My master is in for a treat," she murmured with a secretive smile.

Sick girl. What did they do to her to make her accept her fate so meekly? By the gods he didn't believe in – *not even you Murphy,* no matter what the mercenary handbook stated – he wanted to cheer. If she took to her fate with this alien slug so calmly and willingly, wait until he gave her a more palatable option. Or was that edible? She did have the plumpest lips, perfect in shape and size for…

Later. He'd ponder their use later. Right now, he needed to concentrate. A rich alien such as this one wouldn't dismiss his guards without having backups in place, alarms he could activate possibly with just a thought. Makl needed to be ready to move lightning quick when his moment came. But no need to hurry, not when there was so much he should still, ahem, *observe*.

Off came the female's remaining veil. Her dark hair lay coiled atop her head in fat ringlets, a few escaping to frame her face. He'd enjoy letting the heavy mass down later and pulling it as he rode her from behind. The silky cloak went next, hitting the floor in a pool of fabric she stepped away from, bringing her tall, willowy frame closer to her new owner, but not quite in reach of the tentacles. She wore an almost sheer gown, another neck to ankle affair, the metallic silver of it thin and camouflaging while at the same time perfectly outlining her humanoid shape. Spinning on her heel, the garment flowed around her, teasing and hugging two high breasts – one less than he usually ordered – revealing and hiding two thighs – which he preferred to three – and hiding whether or not her sex possessed teeth like he'd heard his cousin Jaro joke about.

Surely, even his cousin wasn't crazy enough to bed a female whose sex could bite his manhood off? Maybe he should have researched human physiology a bit more. But then again, if Jaro and Tren were brave enough to get between a pair of human thighs, so was he!

"Take the robe off," rumbled the fat alien.

Order or not, she didn't obey. She whirled instead, dipping into a dance that saw her wispy gown swirling out and tucking against her, a mesmerizing routine that with each turn revealed flesh as she undid enclosures in strategic spots, a professional strip tease if he'd ever seen one.

A virgin with lessons in seduction, and not from just any teacher. Makl recognized the pattern of the Khiuya dance, a rare, erotic art taught to only a choice few. No wonder she went for such a high price. Not only was her kind not often seen in the galaxy, it seemed this pale human underwent the rare education to become a true courtesan. This mission was getting better and better.

Faster and faster, his virgin twirled. More ivory skin appeared as fabric whipped in swaying arcs as her arms and body gyrated. The alien grunted, his tentacles flailing in excitement as she simulated a mating dance, one that affected the silent, watching Makl. Throbbing hard, he couldn't look away, or stem his rising lust. He quietly adjusted his cock in his leather pants then readied himself. *Forget the female and take care of the target.*

Just as she spun, her back to the alien, the hint of her buttocks showing, Makl struck. Two quick cuts, downward left, crossing over right, and the corpulent being slid into pieces on the floor.

Not one of his more noble assassinations, but given the door didn't disintegrate in a barrage of laser gunfire aimed his way? The right choice.

He didn't hide before the slave twirled back. Her movements stumbled to a halt. She stared at the floor in shock and stepped back from the oozing slime of her recently deceased owner. She swallowed hard.

Makl must have made a noise because up snapped her head. Brown eyes of chocolate – a rare delicacy he'd tasted more than a few times – stared at him in shock. Wiping his blade, he waited for the female to scream – a sound the guards probably expected. He got a gasp. He then waited for his hug, or tearful thank you. Instead, he got, "You fucking idiot. What the hell did you do?"

Blades sheathed, Makl raised a puzzled gaze to the beauty frowning at him. Hands on her hips, legs astride, and her eyes flashing daggers, she didn't look happy with the turn of events. Nor did she look so meek and innocent. Did she not understand he'd given her freedom? From this monster at least. Now, finders keepers, she belonged to him.

"I killed him." He flashed a slow, seductive grin.

She didn't seem impressed. "I see that. Why?"

"I was multitasking," he answered when his formidable smile didn't send her rushing to take back her harsh query and throw herself on her knees to thank him properly.

"Multi what?" His answer flummoxed her. "I think we need to back up a second. Who are you?"

Makl puffed out his chest, tilted his chin, and adopted a pose that people – ahem, okay, his grandmother – assured him made him look positively regal. "I am Makl, first class warrior from the planet Aressotle. Known as the galactic avenger, I'm here to save you from a fate worse than death."

"Never heard of you." She waved a hand dismissively.

"Sure you have."

"Nope."

"Well, now you have the honor. Say hello to the greatest acquisitions expert and deadliest warrior known in the universe." He executed a perfect bow and waited for her to finally show the appreciation he deserved.

She smirked. At him. "A thief and a murderer. How charming."

Why did she not seem in awe? "Nothing as common as that. I only deal in high end items and jobs."

"Stealing is stealing. And as for killing, anyone can do that. It just takes knowing a creature's weakness."

"Exactly." He inclined his head to the oozing heap on the floor. "His was letting his cock dictate common sense."

"Well, on that we agree. What's your soft spot?" Her query held a hint of challenge.

Out puffed his chest. "I don't have one."

"Of course you don't," she agreed, her subtle nod denuding part of a nipple, which drew his eye like a magnet.

Damn it, he fell for her trap. Before he knew it, the slave – who didn't act like either a slave or woman should – held something with a cold metallic muzzle under his chin. How did she acquire a weapon? He'd seen them scan her himself as he hid in the drapery, his cloak blending him into the background.

"Males. All the same. Flash a little nip and they lose all common sense. Now what were we saying, ah yes, how you don't have a weak spot? Care to recant?"

"I don't think you'll do it."

"Yes, I would."

Not given the way she'd looked positively faint at the sight of a corpse. "Nope. I think you're bluffing."

"Really? You know, all I need to do is press this trigger," she whispered, digging the gun into his skin. "And bam, you're dead."

Makl sighed. Really? Did she think him that unskilled? Then again, he had to wonder at her own attributes. "I am beginning to think you're not a virgin."

"What gave it away?"

"For one thing, you're not sucking my cock in gratitude for saving you."

She snorted. "Are the women you're acquainted with really that slutty?"

"Yes. And don't call them slutty. They prefer the term appreciative."

"I'm sure they are for the few minutes it takes."

It took him a moment to catch the insult. "Are you casting aspersion on my manhood?"

"No, your stamina. I have no doubt you're a man. Cocky. Full of himself..." Her free hand reached between his legs and squeezed. "Oh, but surprise, at least you own enough to brag. I guess you get a little credit."

A shame she let go. If she thought him impressive semi-soft wait until she got a hold of him fully hard. "If you're not a virgin, and you're not happy about me killing this pathetic excuse for a being, then what are you? Oh, by the goddess Karma, please tell me you're not part of an intergalactic strike team whose primary purpose is fighting crime?" He couldn't stem his appalled tone.

"Me? Law enforcement?" Her laughter pealed out loud and contagious.

Makl couldn't help but grin, especially since the pistol under his chin wavered. "Guess not. Then why are you here?"

"Same reason you are, I suspect. Money."

"Slaves can't own assets." A stupid observation given he already suspected she wasn't mere chattel either.

"Again with the assumptions." She clucked her tongue. "Are you sure you're not the greatest idiot the galaxy has known?"

Insulted. Again. By a female no less. Mercenary rule number twenty-two; thou shalt not let a female best you, not even in a battle of words. Reassert dominance through any means possible.

One. Two. In a heartbeat, he held the arm with the weapon twisted behind her back, and the other clasped between their bodies. Their touching bodies. He leaned in close. "Did no one ever teach you not to taunt men bigger than you?"

"Actually, my uncle showed me from a young age how to rile men like you up. But it was his sister who taught me how to escape."

Escape? As if he'd let her go. Of course, he'd not counted on her aunt's ploy. The human didn't try to pull away or struggle. Instead, taller than a female should be, she stretched a little higher and caught his lower lip with flat edged white teeth, then sucked it while grinding her lower body against his.

Holy frukx! Instant heat and lust blossomed as she finally caved in to the desire she obviously couldn't contain. About time things started unfolding the way he'd planned. Her wet tongue swiped across his pointed teeth and he opened wide to let her in. She tasted so perfect. Sugary sweet, and she knew how to use her tongue to full advantage, stroking it along his, sucking on it. Groaning into his mouth. Or was he groaning into hers? Did it matter? He inhaled as she exhaled, her sweet breath filling him. His knees wobbled. He sank. Sank right to the floor. Boneless. Blinking. He had only a moment to see her triumphant smile before he fell on his face, drugged.

I am such an idiot.

Chapter Four

Olivia stared at the purple male keeled over on the floor. She didn't feel bad she'd drugged him. After all, he admitted to being a murderer and a thief, but she did wish she could have met him under different circumstances. The man could kiss and while his views bordered on pompous and chauvinistic, he had an entertaining aspect to him that she quite enjoyed. Toss in what felt like a hard body in a shape similar it seemed to her own, and she could just imagine the fun they could have.

However, this wasn't playtime. With a job left to do, a botched one, she might add, she had limited time to salvage what she could and get out.

Heading to a wall panel indistinguishable from the rest but for a small scratch at the bottom, she hit the hidden catch. A door slid open and in sauntered her partner. Appearing like a human-sized dog – minus the collar and bad breath – he made her think of the pooch she'd briefly owned as a child, if that dog wore pants and a shirt, talked, and had paws tipped with stubby, hairy fingers.

"Took you long enough…" Ifruum stepped around her and stopped. "What happened here? Why is your new owner oozing green blood from more parts than he previously owned and a purple merc out cold on the floor?"

She averted her eyes from the cooling puddle. Dead bodies weren't her thing, even alien ones.

"Ignore the purple dude. He's a wanna be hero. He thought he was doing me a favor by killing our mark. I ended up using the gas on him when he got fresh with me."

"Fresh as in…?"

"None of your business. What are we going to do?"

"Well, this sucks." Ifruum frowned, his furry snout scrunching. "I was hoping to keep this mark alive because he's so gullible and rich. Aw well. At least we got our credits before the assassin took him out. We should get you out of here before someone tries to arrest you for murder."

Arrested for murder in the Obsidian Galaxy? She almost giggled at the inanity of it.

"Did you see him type in the codes?" Ifruum asked as he ran a device over the many fingertips of the downed alien, catching the distinctive whorls and patterns.

"Every single one. He might have many tentacles, but he didn't count on my eidetic memory."

"Excellent. I've got what I need then. Let's go."

Ifruum headed to the opening in the wall.

"What about him?" she asked, pointing to the limp purple body on the floor. Despite herself, she couldn't seem to ignore the alien with the incredible lips and kissing technique.

He mistook her query. "How forgetful of me. You're right. I guess we should frisk him. You never know what we might find." Dropping to his haunches, Ifruum's paws patted down the guy, pulling forth a holographic tablet and not much else.

Olivia kept staring at the silvery cloak, which she happened to notice encased a very nice body.

She kicked her own downed garment into a puddle of green goo. "Can you help me get his cape? Mine got alien guts on it." Ifruum didn't even turn to see as he tugged the shimmery fabric free and handed it to her. Swirling it around her shoulders, Olivia couldn't help but inhale the scent. Mmm. Clean and soapy with a hint of cologne, a musky aroma that sent a shiver through her.

"Other than weapons, the fellow travels light." Ifruum stood. "I wonder if anyone hired him for the kill? I hadn't heard about any hits ordered."

"Does it really matter?" she asked, anxious to leave.

"I was just wondering in case we could lay claim to the credits. But, then again, he makes the perfect alibi. I guess it would be foolish to get too greedy."

"What do you think they'll do to him?" she asked, as they strode back to the secret entrance they'd paid a fortune to find out about.

Ifruum shrugged. "Kill him. Jail him. He's a pretty boy. They might even sell him to a brothel to make some money."

A whore? Somehow, Olivia couldn't see the cocky male allowing that. But, his fate wasn't her concern. They'd gotten what they came for. Time to leave before someone caught on to their scam and came after them. As for leaving the purple dude to take the blame, technically, he had done the crime. Olivia upheld her part of the bargain. Not her fault the alien died – leaving her a rich woman.

With this heist, she and Ifruum ensured their retirement. *Life of leisure here I come.* No more dirty jobs, no more prep work, just relaxation and fun.

She should have known better than to tempt Murphy. Stupid adopted uncle was always looking after her, whether she liked it or not.

*

Bested by a female, a human one at that. It still rankled almost two days later. Forget the fact she'd left Makl to take the blame for his kill – one good deed did not forgive her – taking his cloak and not even molesting him before employing her dastardly plan? Unforgivable!

How did she resist my kiss? She'd enjoyed it. He knew she had. There was faking it with slobber and moans, then there was her reaction – short pants, feverish hot skin, genuine growls of bliss. Oh, and the musky scent of her arousal. She should have been thinking of the pleasure ahead, not plotting his demise.

At least Makl got a mention in the local news. If only they'd mentioned his name rather than referring to him as the purple killer. He'd call in the details himself later and make sure the news channels got their facts straight. It would make the piece on his eventual escape and the heist of the jewels as his crowning touch all the sweeter.

And then, he'd track down the human who tricked him. *Once I find her…* He'd throw her scrumptious frame over his shoulder and abduct her, mercenary style. He had it all planned out – plotted in between his arrest and his short court appearance where a three-breasted, aqua-skinned female judge tried him for unsanctioned murder. By rote, he flirted with the older, portly matron perched atop the towering podium as he pictured his retaliation on the human. He'd tie her to his bed. Strip her slowly, then...

The judge rendered her verdict with a flutter of her dozen eyelids and a glance below his waist. Makl smiled back with all his teeth showing. The game was not yet lost. Sure, he'd let his cock rule his head and it almost cost him his life. Lucky for him, his pretty face, once again, saved the day. The judge decided to make him pay for his crimes by selling him to a local brothel. But before he'd get sent to his new home, he needed to wait for them to process the paperwork.

In the meantime, he spent the waiting period in a less than sumptuous jail. Alone. The laws on this planet tended to mete justice quickly and permanently. So it was with surprise he heard the key jangle in his lock. He wasn't supposed to transfer for another day or so, which meant he was getting company. Makl opened a lazy eyelid just as the door to his cell slid open and another unlucky prisoner was sent to join him.

"I demand a lawyer," growled a familiar barbarian voice. "That wasn't a trial. I never even got to defend myself."

Not surprising, the pigs lugging the object of his fantasies into the room didn't answer. She glared at them as they stomped out and locked the heavy metal door.

Well. Well. When he'd initially woken in his prison, he'd cursed himself for not following the mercenary code. Thankfully, the goddess Karma did so love him. Loved him so much, she brought him a present.

Glad now that he'd bided his time in the cell, knowing escape was only a few galactic units away, Makl wanted to rub his hands with glee. Alive. A bit of fame under his belt. Escape near at hand, and now, sweet revenge.

It took only a moment for him to pin his new cellmate, a certain human female – who wasn't a virgin, dammit! – against the cold metal wall. She looked different, her long coiled locks of before gone in favor of a short, spiked hairstyle. But new haircut or not, he recognized her. His not so virgin human.

He leaned his face in close to hers, almost closing his eyes in delight as her soft, flowery fragrance enveloped him. "We meet again, not so innocent one."

"If it isn't the purple prankster, or was that punster?" She cocked her head and smirked.

"It's the galactic avenger."

"Avenger of what?"

Staring at her lips, he lost focus at her question. "What do you mean of what?"

"What are you avenging?"

"Nothing."

"Then how did you choose the name?"

He frowned at her. "Why does it matter?"

"Never mind. If you want people to know who you are, though, you really should get a uniform or something."

"Are you mocking me?"

"Asks the guy who is trying to be like some super space pirate."

"You compare me to a pirate?" He arched a brow. "Is it because I'm dashing? Bold? Handsome? Rakish appearing?"

"I was thinking more of unkept, unwashed, and stealer of things not belonging to him."

"You forgot ravisher of females."

"I don't know if it's considered ravishing when you pay for it." The sweet smile she bestowed for some reason irritated him.

"Anyone ever mention you're most annoying?"

Russet lips parted further. "Thank you. I was trained by the best. I can give you his number if you'd like? You know, to hone your skills."

Had she…? She wouldn't dare! Frukx it all, she had. She'd insulted him. Accused him of not being as good as her. Worse, until he bested her, she was.

"I should kill you," he growled to even the score. "You left me there to take the blame."

"Well, you did murder that poor, defenseless alien."

He had and didn't regret it one bit. Apparently, though, she didn't see his chivalrous deed in the same light. So, he needed to give her a good reason for his actions. Females loved a hero, and given what he'd suffered – a catch up on his sleep, terrible food resulting in the loss of the few meteoric units he'd gained on his last space trip – she should feel guilty for her treatment of him. Despite his motives, he'd saved her. Never mind she appeared to have her own plan. He acted first. "Can you really call it murder when I did it to save you?"

She choked. "Ha. Save me? What a crock. You did it to steal me, more than likely."

He shrugged and let his lip curl as she saw through him. "That too. It is what I do. Acquire precious items."

"Why?"

"What do you mean why?"

She cocked her head and peered at him seriously. "Why me? I mean, why go through the trouble? You don't seem like the slaver type."

"Can't a male save a female in distress?" He cocked a brow and waggled it.

She didn't fall for it and yet, that same look got him second servings of dessert at home all the time. "You don't strike me as the altruistic type."

"I'm not. Altruism is for the weak." A mercenary rule? Of course. An expansion of rule number one.

"So why come after me?"

"Because I've always wanted to bed a barbarian virgin." A dream he now had to postpone, damn her.

A very odd snort came from her. "That has got to be the stupidest thing you've said so far."

"No, it's not." He frowned as he caught the circle she trapped him in. "I'm sure I've said stupider." Like just then. What was it about this woman that turned him into a bumbling idiot? He tried to recapture his usual suaveness. "I saw you. I was horny. I came and got you. How was I supposed to know you lied on your resume? I should sue you for false advertising. I would have never ended up in this cell if not for your 'Hey look at me, I am a rare, certified virgin.' "

Her jaw dropped, wide enough to insert… She screeched. "Are you serious? Oh my God. You are. Unbelievable. And just…no, still unbelievable. There has to be something more. A better reason. Surely you are not that shallow or stupid. It can't just be for sex. You are obviously good-looking enough to find a female to bed. Or at least rich enough to pay one to fake it. Coming after me so you could pop my cherry? That's insane."

"Well, it wasn't the only reason." But it made for better watching. Makl peeked up at the camera that recorded their fight.

"Aha! I knew there was another reason. What treasure did the rich dude have hidden?"

"Only one item. You."

"You won't get me to believe you went through all that trouble just to steal me."

"But I did. From the moment I saw you, I knew I needed you."

Funny how the honest claim made her pupils dilate and her lips part. A momentary softness that quickly disappeared. "Need me for what? And don't say sex."

Okay, he wouldn't say it, but he'd think it because despite her non-virgin status, he still wanted to get between her thighs and make her scream his name. "I was tasked with bringing a human back to my aunt."

"You know that just raises more questions than answers because you, of course, purposely don't mention for what."

"And ruin the surprise?"

"I hate surprises."

"Funny, because you gave me quite the one just a few days ago. Why don't you answer a few questions first yourself if you're so keen on knowing more, such as what you were doing masking as a virgin slave in the first place?"

"Who says it was a mask?"

He snorted.

Her lips tilted. "Okay, maybe I wasn't a slave, but you heard the doctor. I'm a virgin, or are you putting my cherry in doubt?" She gave him a pretty pout.

He didn't fall for it this time. "If you're a maiden, then I have balls that hang."

Up shot her delicately curved brows. "You don't have balls under your cock?"

Why the shock? He frowned. "Of course not. No warrior race would ever have them that vulnerable to damage."

"Interesting."

And no, he didn't swell because her gaze veered south of his waistband. "You still haven't answered me. Why play the part of slave?" he reminded with a little shake.

"You had a job and so did I. I get sold to the highest bidder. He pays for me, and I slip away before he can act, richer than before."

"You've pulled this con before?"

She pursed her lips and blew. "Well, duh. Of course, never on such a large scale before. Usually, we tackle smaller marks. This was our first big one. I have to admit, up until you showed up, it was going perfect."

"Perfect until they caught you."

"No, it was the perfect scam. We got away clean. But my partner made the mistake of reading the notes we stole from you."

Makl straightened at her implication. "You went after my target?" And who was this mysterious partner? A male he needed to kill or a female, a bisexual female who would like to join in?

"Yeah. We went after the stupid diamond and failed. If it's any consolation, your plan didn't work. The jeweler had an extra layer of security no one knew about. I got caught." Her lips turned down in a pout of epic proportions.

A chuckle rumbled from him, a laugh that saw him releasing her and stepping away. "Then I guess I owe you my thanks."

She rubbed her neck as she shot him a wary gaze. "Then we're even now?"

"Oh not quite, but I'll save my revenge for later when the time is more appropriate. We are not exactly alone, if you understand my meaning." He peered up at the camera. The human frowned.

"For a lawless galaxy, they're awfully strict," she complained. "Cops. Judges. Cells. I would have found more corruption on Polza."

Polza, the planet of rules where the job of enforcing the millions of edicts was an industry unto itself. Thankfully, bribery was a common currency there. "But Polza lacks the riches and the notoriety. I don't see why you're so upset. You'll now be infamous."

"I'd have preferred to stay anonymous. I don't get you. You're awfully chipper for a man about to discover if there is a God."

"I know gods exist. Pains in the buttocks, most of them. But I am not scheduled to die. The female judge sold me to her favorite brothel. I expect she'll be my first client."

The human female blinked, then shuddered. "Oh, now there's a mental image I didn't need."

Makl knew better than to imagine it. Besides, his mind couldn't focus on anything other than the pale, two-legged beauty pacing the cell, the folds of his cloak tangling in her legs. Brazen chit. She not only left him to take the blame, she'd stolen his clothing as well. "Once you get past the teeth, it's not bad. And the slime washes off." He couldn't help but laugh as disgust twisted her features.

"How can you joke about it?"

"Come here if you want to know." He crooked a finger.

She crossed her arms. "I don't think so."

"Suit yourself then." He sat with his back against the wall, closed his eyes, and proceeded to ignore her.

It didn't take her long to lose patience. "How can you just sit there? Aren't you even going to try and escape?"

"Escape? From this most secure of cells? Impossible." He didn't even look at the camera as he made the claim.

She blew out a breath. "Not the answer I was looking for. I hope you enjoy your new career as a hooker."

She tried to rile him up and get him to do something rash. Nice ploy, also a mercenary rule he well knew. "Oh, I don't imagine I'll be there long."

"Whorehouse security is even tighter than that in these cells."

"A matter of opinion."

"So you're not even going to try and escape from here?" She gestured to their room.

"Why bother?"

"Then I'm wasting time talking to you," she grumbled, whirling away from him. She paced the cell, eyeing it's every nook and cranny. A shame she didn't drop his cloak while doing it. He could have used the show. But dressed as she was, he made do with his vivid imagination. Of course, he couldn't see why she tried to squeeze her head between impossibly tight bars, or why she kept mumbling about spoons. Did she plan to eat her way out? If so, he could help her, eat her out, that was.

"May I ask what you are doing?" he asked when she scrabbled on the floor, nose to the stone.

"Looking for a way to escape. Unlike you, the female judge did not like me and sentenced me to death. They're just waiting for a slot to open up so they can put the show on stage and sell some tickets."

Death? Served her right. Only human around or not, the female was a menace. The laws he lived by said she should die for what she'd done. Revenge screamed this was justice. His rules said better her than him. But his cock – too full of itself and most of the blood powering his brain – and his practical side disagreed. *I can still use her.* He sighed. Frukx it all. Irritating human or not, there was only one thing to do.

"Come here." He crooked a finger.

"Why?"

"Must you always question?"

"Yes."

"You forgot to phrase it as a query."

Her lips twitched. "Are you wanting me close so you can throttle me?"

No, but he owned a body part in need of a good throttling or choking. Either would do. "Again with the questions. Frukx it all, woman, I've had it." Up he sprang from the bed. In a moment, he once again held her pinned against the wall. "Why can't you just listen to a male when he speaks?"

When she started her harangue, he leaned in close and whispered in her ear. "Don't stop talking, but listen carefully. I'll help you escape."

She, of course, shut up.

"Stupid barbarian. I should teach you a female's proper place. The only thing you're good for."

"And what would that be?" she snapped.

"Everyone knows a female's position when in the presence of male should be on her knees!" he shouted triumphantly. "Prepare to choke on your punishment, human."

This time, the light of understanding clicked and she launched into a rant the likes his Aunt Muna would have applauded. He used it to cover his own words. "They're watching us, so we can't let on we're planning our exit."

"But how will you make me, you scoundrel? Gag me and I shall bite it off. I dare you to take me by force. Or are you just loud noise?"

Under the guise of something else, she asked her questions and he replied in kind.

"Loud noise? I'll show you. I can conquer anything. Even the lock on your portal. I have the strength and the tool to force my way."

"Figures you'd rely on force." She tossed her head. "I'll fight. Do anything I can."

Fight? Against armed guards. She might try, but it was obvious to him she wasn't trained to act in a deadly fashion. He kept up his oblique speech and hoped she followed. "You can perhaps escape me on one condition."

"What's that?" She eyed him suspiciously.

"You help me with my *errand*." He waggled a brow.

She fell out of character, but to anyone watching their conversation still revealed nothing of the plan they hatched. "What kind of errand? Because I am not donating any body parts for eating or science."

"Your body will remain intact." He thought.

"I am not fucking you either."

So she thought. "Female, I wanted sex with the demure virgin, not whatever you call yourself."

"My name is Olivia."

Odd name. But then again, look where she originated from. "I am Makl."

"Galactic hijacker, I know. So no sex, no donation of body parts, or pain. Will I survive what you plan?"

"That is my understanding."

"Then I agree."

"You do? Aren't you going to ask me what the job entails?"

She shrugged. "If I don't like it, I'll leave."

"That might not be as easy as you think."

"I'm sure I'll figure out a way. So now what, oh great galactic Barney."

"Who?"

She hid a smile. "No one. So Makl, what's next?"

"Now you pay!" He winked out of sight of the camera. She almost gave it away.

"Ooh, I am so scared."

"You should be. I've been told my size is almost monstrous. Prepare for the ravishment of your life. But first, less clothes."

"I don't think so."

"Hand the cloak over, human." Did she have to defy him at every turn? Yes. It was one of her charming traits. Lips pursed, she swirled his cape from her shoulders into his outstretched hand. With a flourish, he tossed it on the pallet. "You learn quickly. Just listen when I speak and you'll soon know your place," he advised.

"Doing what?"

He mashed his mouth down on to hers before she could ask any more frukxing questions and give the plan away. To his relief, she didn't bite his tongue off. And this time, he remained upright.

Chapter Five

Taken by surprise, Olivia didn't have time to think, but she certainly felt when Makl kissed her with a sudden passion. Unlike earlier, when she concentrated on getting him to lower his guard so she could gas him with the capsule hidden in her tooth, this time, she had nothing to fight him with. Other than her tongue, and that proved more pleasurable than effective in getting him to stop his delicious kiss.

Damn, the alien, so like a real man, attracted her. He appealed to her senses. From his sculpted body to his bantering, she couldn't deny he brought her to life, stimulating her in all the right spots. And she meant *all*. He sure packed a wallop of a kiss! Olivia was by no means innocent. She'd put her curiosity about sex to the test years ago and remained for the most part unimpressed, but she should perhaps revise that attitude given with just a single embrace, Makl raised her blood temperature to boiling – in a good way. But, hormones humming or not, French kissing wouldn't help them escape.

In between pants, she whispered. "What's the plan?"

"Just keep following my lead," he muttered back before kissing her anew in a thorough way that left talking unfeasible.

Odd how his lead meant her tongue getting knotted with his. The tips of her breasts, crushed against his chest, peaked. Her sex moistened. She found herself swaying into him, rubbing and pressing, trying to get closer. His large hands roamed her back, massaging her spine with hard fingers that dug in just right and then traveled down the length of her frame to cup her buttocks. She gasped when he lifted her, fitting her sex tightly against the hard bulge at his groin. Evidence of his desire rubbed decadently along the front of her mound.

She moaned. Insane. Crazy. Hard to care. She'd never lost herself in a moment like this before. Just let herself feel… She vocalized her pleasure.

"That's it. Moan a little louder," he coaxed.

His murmured words broke a little of the spell, enough she opened her eyes and saw him reach behind him to grab and throw his cloak. He aimed for the camera in the corner. The silky fabric caught the tip of the spying device and slid to the floor. Great. Someone hand her the stupid award of the hour. She'd given him the nice warm cape to use as a lens cover so he could get into her pants. *How could I forget for a moment about my arrest, pending sentence, and everything else just because a perfect stranger put his tongue down my throat?*

What sucked even more than her idiotic reaction to his kiss? She still would prefer to kiss him than deal with the bleak situation in which she found herself. Was it too much to ask for just a little peace and quiet? Why hadn't she taken the retirement instead of going after the treasure? Why was she letting him melt her with the nibbles against her throat? He caused her situation. He promised to get her out. That meant no more kissing.

About to launch into a tirade, she almost bit her tongue instead as his lips moved from her neck to the lobe of her ear, nipping the tender flesh while his warm breath fluttered in the shell.

"Pretend you're enjoying this," he hissed. "Unless you've changed your mind about escaping?"

She faked a gasp and clutched his hair – tight enough to make most men wince – and yanked his head down so she could pretend to give his ear the same erotic treatment.

"It's hard to pretend when I don't feel a thing."

"Liar." He blew the hot word into her ear. Forget controlling the shudder sweeping through her.

Okay, so it felt good. It didn't change anything. "Sex isn't going to melt those bars no matter how hot."

His low chuckle sent shivers down her spine. "At least you admit it would be hot. But alas, this is just part of the plan to escape."

She snorted, but didn't stop her nibbling of his skin – he did taste quite delicious. Faking it wasn't proving the chore she pretended.

"Oh, my sweet barbarian," he groaned, taking a step back. Louder, "Never fear. I won't let you die a virgin."

"Excuse me?" She could have caught a lot of things considering how low her jaw dropped.

"A sweet thing like your deflowering should take place on the softest of linens. Just you and I, naked. Skin to skin. My mighty cock cleaving your most tender of places."

A giggle left her. Then a snort. About to mock him, she caught a slight shake of his head. She adjusted her words. "How romantic?" She couldn't help the questioning lilt.

"Romantic? Alas, with time running out, we shall have to make do with what we have. I just wish we had more privacy." He winked at her as he gestured to the room, more specifically, the cloak at his feet.

And she finally got her head out of her pussy and caught on. "Oh, my purple stud muffin. You say the hottest things." She whipped her shirt off, leaving her clad only in a thin bandeau across her breasts. With a seemingly negligent toss, she flung her top; the hem of the neckline and lighter fabric caught the edge of the camera and hung. Now the guards watching would have to rely on sound only, which explained Makl's outrageous speech. Or at least she hoped that wasn't how he spoke to his lovers. Not that she intended to find out. Great kisser or not, he'd only embraced her as part of his plan. And she'd gone along with greater acting skill than she realized she owned. The wet panties and flushed skin were a nice touch. Maybe she should look into going on stage as an actress?

However, the show wasn't done, not if Makl's oration was any indication. "Yes, you decadent barbarian. Bare yourself for me that I might taste the fruit of your body."

"Lick me like a bonbon," she cried. She joined in, grasping their need to cover their actions. She still didn't understand what he planned. As he scrounged through the folds of his cloak, he kept up a running commentary.

"What are you doing on your knees, human? I am much too big and thick for your sweet, precious mouth. Ah. Ah. Yes, you wicked temptress." He caught her gaze with the last word.

She rolled her eyes at his wide grin, but played along as he pulled something out of a cloak she could have sworn didn't own a single pocket. "You." Pursing her lips, she made a slurping noise. "Ain't seen nothing." Suctioning sound. "Yet. My vagina is even tighter than my mouth. Wetter. And waiting for you."

Did his eyes cross? She couldn't have said for certain as Makl dropped his baton with a muttered curse. "Ooh, watch those teeth, my lovely. My big purple monster is perhaps too much for your small mouth."

Oh, that made her choke for real. "Oh, let me keep trying. You taste so yummy, but goodness, you're just sooooo big." Olivia put a finger in her mouth and pretended to gag. Makl grabbed the rod from the floor and shook with silent laughter, his icy eyes crinkling at the corners.

"Big and hard, just for you, my sumptuous barbarian. Now bend over that I might plow you with my mighty sword."

Plow? She mouthed the word at him with a wrinkled nose and he grinned as he extended the short rod into a baton, the snick of metal clicking into place covered by her pretend noises of wet pleasure.

"Oh. Oh. Oh. Yes. Take it, human. Take all of my mighty cock."

Olivia fought hard not to laugh as she replied in kind. "Harder. Yes. Yes. Harder. I love the feel of you banging my uterus. You are so big. Yes! Yes!"

It seemed their playacting bore results. The guards didn't even attempt to keep quiet as they came rushing down the hall, booted feet thumping. Eager bastards. She curled her lip at their predictable need for a firsthand view of the action.

Makl twirled the silvery cloak around his shoulders and beckoned her to join him. She hesitated. And he disappeared. Literally.

What the fuck? She stuttered to a halt right in the middle of her fake orgasm. *Where did he go? Don't tell me that damned cloak was a teleporter and I never figured it out.* But if he was gone, why could she still hear him faking it? She yelped as a disembodied hand emerged from nowhere and yanked her against a broad chest.

"Keep screaming," he admonished between his own yells of bliss. Not so easy anymore when the scent of him – feel of him – flooded her senses. Her moans turned breathy and the heat of before returned full force, focusing on the bundle of nerves between her thighs. Pressed tight against him, each slight friction of their bodies seemed to rub against it, sending small shockwaves through her. When her breath caught and she went silent, he yelled, "I'm coming." Then once again, meshed his mouth to hers, absorbing any sound she might have made when the door to their prison slid open. A brief embrace just long enough to keep her quiet while the guards entered the cell with a puzzled, "Where the frukx are they?"

Spinning her away from him, Makl went into motion. Out shot his leg, his foot sweeping behind one guard's leg. The bar he swung at the other thug in uniform knocked his pistol clear – in the opposite direction of Olivia who watched in frozen fascination. Despite her upbringing, she seldom encountered true violence first hand. It both fascinated and repelled. The power Makl displayed, the force behind each jab... When he whirled, his fist connected with a solid thud to the fleshy jowl of the guard. Down went the alien in an unconscious heap. That she could handle, but it was the wrench of the neck after that sent her stumbling back.

He killed him!

Shocked at the violence, she never saw the danger. She yelped as an arm wrapped around her from behind. She clawed at the rough fabric covering the thick appendage to no avail. She needed rescue, yet Makl fought his own battle.

The lessons Ifruum had her take – more like forced on her despite her pouting – took over. Down went her foot, flexible shoes against hard, tungsten-toed boots. Yeah, the guy didn't even flinch. She winced even before she flung her head back, expecting the denser noggin that collided with her head. Self-defense was great in theory, but in the grand scheme of things, fragile-skinned humans didn't stand a chance against the better armored races.

Although, Makl seemed an exception to the rule. His exterior seemingly just as thin-skinned, her purple killer spun with a crazy grace. Jumping up, spinning, his body contorting in ways that defied belief and gravity. Another guard, a big fucking brute, dropped.

None of which helped Olivia. The open cell door gaped, a barely panting Makl in front of it. Olivia, however, dangled off the ground in the grip of the one guard still standing. She knew in Makl's place what she would have chosen.

He surprised her, though. Makl turned around. Lips split in a wild grin, eyes shining with a savage brightness, he displayed pointed teeth – sharp, sharklike teeth. "Let the girl go and I'll give you a head start."

There went her ability to breathe as the arm around her neck tightened.

"The female stays."

Shaking his head, Makl let out a dramatic sigh. "Why does no one ever take the head start?" Faster than she could follow, he sprang at them. Makl swung his slim bar and it slammed across the knuckles of the smelly alien holding her. With a yelp, he let go. She hit the floor and struggled to take in a wheezing breath.

Long, lean legs straddled her, Makl standing over her as he took care of the last guard. She covered her head lest boots trample her, but somehow, she remained untouched. A thump and she peeked through her fingers to see the sightless gaze of the last guard.

Violence came so easily to Makl. She swallowed the bile threatening to rise. "Did you have to kill them all?"

"Mercenary rule number four. Never leave any of the enemy behind you alive lest they come back to kill you."

"There are mercenary rules?"

"Yes. But now's not the time to learn them. I'll loan you the book later if you'd like."

He owned a book? "You can read?" She couldn't help the sarcastic retort, her mind's way of dealing with the trauma around her.

"And write. Is now really the time for me to list my extensive accomplishments?"

"What do you know, you're not just pretty." She patted him on the cheek.

He growled. "I don't know how I ever mistook you for an innocent virgin. Come. We don't have much time before our escape is discovered."

He held out his hand and she looked at it, feeling once again that an omen hung over her head, a giant blinking sign that warned she stood on the brink of change. *If I go with him…* She might just end up in his bed finishing the act they started – *I'd be sleeping with a certifiable killer.* If she didn't, she'd meet up with Ifruum at their prearranged meeting spot in case of calamity and retire on her earnings.

How boring. Nothing like the pulse-pounding action she'd experienced since she'd met Makl. Did she have to remove herself to a life of tranquility right away? *After all, I did promise to help him with something if we escaped.* As fellow thieves of a sort, didn't their code have some rule about honor among…?

About to slip her hand into his in silent acceptance of her fate, a siren blazed to life. "Frukx it all. I didn't expect them to notice the guards' demise so quick. I've no time to wait on your feminine games. We leave now." In true caveman style, he upended her over his shoulder despite her squealed, "Don't you dare."

"Oh, stuff it. A deal is a deal. I told you I needed your help. You agreed so long as we escaped. Congratulations. We're escaping. Now, make it good for the cameras, would you? I've got a reputation to create."

"A reputation based on molesting and kidnapping fellow convicts?" she grumbled as she squirmed, not because he told her to, but because she didn't enjoy being carted about like a sack of potatoes. She also squirmed because she'd never had someone toss her over a shoulder with such effortless ease and as shoulders went, his was quite nice.

"Molesting? Ha. You wish. Anyone could tell you enjoyed yourself."

"I was faking it."

"Only parts of it. Or do I need to throw you up against a wall and show you just how much you didn't fake?"

Please do. "Don't you dare."

"Dare? I love a challenge." His hand crept up her thigh, about to make him a quick winner to his claim.

"Are you insane? Now's not the time. We'll get caught."

"Then tell the truth. You liked it."

Why did it matter? His hand moved up an inch. Her heart thumped faster. If she didn't say anything, would he make good on this threat? His fingers crept closer and her cleft moistened. Damn him. "Maybe I liked it a little."

"A lot."

"Don't push it."

"I won't, until you beg for it. And you will." He said the last with a sensual leer as he set her on her feet.

"You wish."

"I know. Now, take out that camera, would you?" He handed her a gun, which he pulled out of a pocket in the cloak, a gun she could have sworn didn't exist. She'd felt every inch of that fabric. Passed metal detectors. Where was he getting all the stuff from?

Taking the gun, she checked the safety and the indicator level, which showed it fully charged. "How do you know I can shoot?"

"A scammer like yourself has to know how to protect herself somehow. Since hand-to-hand isn't your thing, I assume it's guns. Or knives. But, given you lack calluses and the fact you get squeamish at the sight of a bit of blood, I'm going to guess firearms."

How surprisingly astute of him – maybe a little smarter than she gave him credit for. As she aimed and took fire at the devices manning this stretch of hallway, he bent over, giving her a very nice view of his ass. She couldn't help but ask, "What the hell are you doing now?"

"With them blinded, it's time to foil our pursuers, of course, and buy us some time." Up came a grate in the floor, along with a knife, which he used to shear a lock off her head.

"Hey!"

"It'll grow back." He wedged the hair between the grate and floor, leaving an obvious trail. Then he caught her hand and dragged her close.

"What is it with you and personal space?"

"In order for the cloak to work, we have to be under it."

"That doesn't explain why your hand is on my boob."

He squeezed. "Because I like it there."

So did she, but that was beside the point. "What's next?"

"Now, we go back in the direction we came from."

"What?"

"Let them split up where we took the cameras out and waste their time looking in the wrong places. They don't know about my cloak's abilities and won't expect us to return in that direction."

"Or so you hope. That's crazy."

"Shhh. We're in camera range. Stay close." Damn him. She clamped her lips tight and trusted he knew what he did. But the first chance she got, away she'd flee. Promise or not, the guy was a whack job. A cute whack job, but still, she had enough dealing with one crazy partner without getting involved with a second.

Back up the hall they tread, trusting in the invisibility of the cloak, keeping silent lest the vigilant cameras catch their subterfuge. When the tread of boots came toward them, the urge to run almost took her out from under the cloak. As if sensing her need for flight, Makl tucked them into an alcove, muscled frame squishing hers against the wall, his lips brushing against her ear. Despite the situation, his warm, fanning breath did wicked things to her blood pressure.

The hired guards ran past them, their transmitters squawking. *They're in the sewers. Release the kraken."* Or so her translator called whatever this planet had that passed for one.

Fucking seriously? Mental note to self: never visit the sewers on this planet.

Coast clear again, onwards they went, past their cell and the dead guards, their flight hampered by their need to remain out of sight under a cloak meant for one. Thankfully, they didn't have much farther to go. Passing the empty guard station, they hit some stairs, which ended in a locked door.

This she could handle. "Got any picks in your pockets?"

"We don't have time for that," said the male who'd never seen her in action. Before Olivia could show off her unlocking skills, Makl pulled out a laser pistol and shot the control panel. The door whooshed open and a new alarm wailed to life.

"What was the point in hiding all the way here if you were going to do that?" she complained as he dragged her through the portal.

"The few extra galactic units we gained as a head start might be needed later. Now, follow closely. I'll need my hands free for the next little bit as we might have to fight to make it to my ship."

"Which will never clear the dock. They'll have it clamped down tighter than the chastity belt I had to wear as part of my ruse."

He stumbled. "I would have liked to have seen that."

"I'll bet you would."

"Distract me later with the stories. Follow and prepare to be amazed as I single-handedly save your delicate human skin and escape this cursed planet."

"I'll believe it when I see it." But even she had to admit, the more she saw of Makl – and despite his flirting demeanor – the more she realized he hid a cunning mind. However, did he have enough skill to get them out of here?

If anyone could get them out of this, it would be Ifruum, her friend and teacher, but since her mentor seemed to have left her to her own devices, she'd have to make do with her purple killer.

Uncle Murphy save them both.

Chapter Six

I need to get away from here and off planet. Easier said than done, and if by himself, Makl would give it odds of around fifty percent for accomplishing it alive. Dragging along a human, who winced when he killed to protect? Bound to either get him shot into pieces or catapulted into fame.

It seemed his pretty barbarian, while cool and collected in situations she'd scouted and planned for, didn't do so well when confronted with too much pressure – and violence. That or his awesome kiss still had her wits addled. He preferred to think the latter because it sure scrambled his thought process for a few moments. Oh, the temptation to ravish her, audience, danger, or not. Next time, maybe he wouldn't stop.

Enough. He mustn't think of sex – most specifically with *her* – right now. He needed a clear head to make it through the net of guards and mercenaries probably headed his way. Alone, he could have probably melted away and blended in to the crowd, but with a distinctive human in tow, he would have appreciated some help. If only he'd spent more time looking for a travel companion, a sidekick of sorts, to provide outside support during such situations. A partner to…

A warm breeze fluttered overhead as an aircar dropped from the defined aerial street and hovered. He peered up, expecting to see a strobe light flick on and the security force blare its orders. Instead, from the open door on the side of the vehicle, a ladder unraveled, its metal limbs unfolding and clacking into place.

What in the universe?

"Get in!" a voice shouted. A furry face poked from the opening of the floating car and a paw waved.

Shoving him aside, Olivia scrambled to grab hold and clamber up.

He grabbed her leg in an attempt to hold her back. "What are you doing?"

Kicking free, she turned his way and rolled her eyes. "I'd say it was obvious. I'm escaping. I knew if anyone could save me, it would be Ifruum. Although, you gave it a nice try, purple. Are you coming?"

Coming? I hope to soon, was his leering thought as he stared up at her waggling buttocks, her tight slacks contouring her shape nicely as she clambered up the suspended ladder. If only she wore a skirt, with no undergarments. He would have enjoyed a peek.

Sirens increased in treble and he snapped out of his drooling state – with a mental reminder to garb her in a dress as soon as possible. Grasping at the rungs, he muscled his way up the ladder to her. They didn't have far to climb as the craft began reeling them in. Soon enough, they left the prison and horns behind and sat in plush chairs. Above the city they zoomed, just another speck of traffic. Makl didn't relax, eyeing instead the furry male who listened to Olivia's severely edited version of their escape.

What in the universe is it? Makl couldn't say he recognized what race Olivia's companion belonged to. Floppy-eared, his nose black and moist, the very tall, shambling carpet possessed a somewhat humanoid shape, covered in hair. Lots of it. Straight in spots, tufted curls in others, and splotchy in hue. The odd creature appeared as if he'd started out brown in color, then for fun, someone flicked a paintbrush at him and gave him blobs of grey, white, and black. Slightly comical in appearance, he looked about as dangerous as a newborn with his first wooden club.

"Who and what are you?" he asked when Olivia finally paused her narrative to take a breath.

Soulful brown eyes turned to peer at him. "If it isn't the mighty Galactic Avenger himself. I am most honored to meet you." Down bowed the fuzzy head as if in admiration.

Makl didn't fall for the act for a second – although he wanted to. "How do you know who I am?"

"Doesn't the whole universe?" Eyes, holding a hint of mirth, rose to meet his.

Mockery. The recipient of it at family functions, Makl knew how to recognize it when he saw it. He just didn't understand it, not from a creature he'd never met before. He stared hard at the talking lintball. Big, innocent orbs blinked.

"Ifruum knows a lot of things," Olivia said, snapping her fingers between them, breaking the stare – a staring contest Makl would have won. "He always knows what to do and who people are. It's his gift."

Somehow, Makl would have wagered it less a gift than people underestimating the seemingly innocent alien. "Since you know who I am, then you also know who I'm related to."

Ifruum's muzzle peeled back in a freakish grin. "Very well, actually. You could say I'm doing this as a favor to them."

Makl pursed his lips in displeasure. "Please don't. I prefer to incur and pay my own debts."

"As you wish." A glint of something, cunning perhaps, or mischief, shone in that disturbing gaze for a moment. Makl frowned.

"So Ifruum, what's the plan? Did you book us a flight out of here?" Olivia asked, as she tugged a clean shirt from a sack at her feet and pulled it on. A shame, because he rather preferred her current look with the tight bandeau outlining her breasts and hinting at the dark valley between.

"Why pay for a ticket when our new friend has a ship to get us out of here and to our next job? As a matter of fact, we've arrived already. I hope you don't mind, I took the liberty of moving your spacecraft before they confiscated it."

Forget just frowning, Makl snapped. "How did you get through my security? For that matter, how did you find my ship? I left it frukxing cloaked and locked."

"Does the how really matter when it suits us?" Ifruum queried, as he guided them into the familiar landing bay, which opened at their approach.

Enough was enough. No more riddles. Makl sprang up, as did Ifruum. Toe to toe, they stood, the furball not tall enough to tower over Makl even if both their heads practically rubbed the ceiling of the car. "The how does matter if you want to live."

"Oh, for God's sake. Stuff the testosterone and stop screwing around. We need to work together if we're going to escape." Olivia came out of her seat and inserted her whole body in front of him. She pushed against his chest.

"He started it," Makl accused.

"Because you can't take it. It's what makes it so much fun." His soon-to-be new carpet didn't even try to hide his mirthful disdain.

Makl growled.

Olivia pressed her palm against his chest, but spoke to her friend. "Ifruum, stop. You're antagonizing him, and Makl tends to kill people he perceives as a threat or annoyance."

"I'd listen to her if I were you."

"He won't harm me." Ifruum didn't appear worried in the slightest.

Idiot. "Don't be so sure," Makl snarled.

"Mercenary rule number eleven."

Don't kill your allies. But, was this pain in his buttock an ally? Let's review. Helped him escape. Knew Olivia. Olivia trusted him. Appeared to have aided him despite his wayward tongue. Damn. There went his new shag rug. Although, ally or not, there were exceptions to the mercenary rule. Perhaps Makl could hope Ifruum broke one of them. He didn't like people knowing his business. Or at least the private parts of it. But he especially hated it when people or other aliens touched his belongings. Makl, as an only child, never had shared well.

"You know the mercenary rules too?" Olivia asked her friend as Makl exited the small craft into his ship's landing bay. He didn't pay attention to the answer as he stomped to a control panel, ready to wrest, physically if need be, control of his ship from the furry interloper. To his surprise, he needed to do nothing as his spacecraft responded to his commands without hesitation.

However, to be sure his new ally hadn't left a surprise, he'd run some diagnostics later.

The door to the bay sealed shut, the cloaking device engaged, but only for the moment. As soon as he had to move through the atmosphere shielding the planet, he'd have to drop it. Darned ship couldn't handle the heat and structural stress of breaking free and invisibility at the same time. *Perhaps I should go shopping for a new ship.* His gambling skills could use the exercise.

Ignoring his passengers, he headed for the bridge at a pace just short of a jog. The ease of their escape tickled his gut. Something told him they'd not seen the last of what the planet That-Didn't-Exist could throw at them. The Obsidian's biggest marketplace and most infamous of cities didn't get its reputation by letting anyone snub her.

Locking himself in to the commanding seat in case things got rough, Makl took manual control – because hands on meant he could blame it on equipment failure if things went wrong – and barked out commands. Olivia entered with Ifruum who immediately sat in the secondary seat and took over the sensors looking for incoming craft or missiles. Given they both had a vested interest in not blowing up, Makl let the fuzzy male work with only part of his attention on him.

"Where to next?" Olivia asked, as she wandered the tight space, gaze darting from electronic panel to panel, not missing a thing, he'd wager.

"I'll let you know as soon as we get out of here."

"I wasn't talking to you," she replied coolly.

"Excuse me?" Makl aimed a stare at her. "We're on my ship now, human. It goes where I say it goes."

"For now."

"Are you threatening mutiny?" He couldn't help the surprise in his tone.

A smirk followed her shrug. "Depends on if I like where we're going."

"You are going where you promised, or have you already forgotten? We had a deal. I help you escape and you come with me to help with something."

"That was before I knew you were a cold-blooded killer."

"We met over a corpse, how did you not figure that out? I told you I did assassinations for a living."

"That's a job for money. You killed those guards in cold blood."

"Um, what's the difference?"

"You could have left them alone."

Ifruum choked.

So did Makl. "I killed someone who would have done the same to me. Who would have murdered you without a second thought."

"One of them was unconscious when you did it! How was he dangerous?"

"He would have woken up. Maybe when we were sneaking back out. Maybe he would have seen or heard something as we went by and shot blindly, hurting or killing us. It's just smart to not leave any of the enemy alive."

"Psycho."

The unexpected compliment took him aback. "You think?" Makl preened. "Would you mind repeating that to my cousin when you meet him?"

"You're out of your mind. And who says I'm meeting your cousin?"

"You did when you promised to give me aid."

"Doing what?" She eyed him with suspicion.

"I thought you didn't care so long as it didn't involve body parts." He enjoyed how her lips pursed at his reminder. Point for him. Now, he needed to concentrate. Motors finally all online, he turned his attention to the jump from planetside to space.

But she wasn't about to let up. "I made that promise under duress when I thought we couldn't escape."

"What? You lied to me?" How totally sexy of her.

"Not exactly. I totally meant it at the time. But a girl has the right to change her mind, especially since the situation has evolved."

"It has. We're no longer stuck in a cell. You are on my ship. You go where I say." For a good spanking if she kept this arguing up.

"Oh just tell her what she wants to know and save yourself the aggravation. Trust me. She's worse than a dog with a bone when she gets going."

Tell her why he needed her? If it were for any other reason, Makl wouldn't hesitate, but honestly –

which he hated – Makl didn't want to say the words aloud. He didn't want to hear the derision. Yet, he didn't have a choice. He'd have to admit what he needed Olivia for eventually. Time to bite the embarrassment bullet. "You really want to know? Fine. My cousin and his wife need a nanny."

Ifruum laughed first. "You want her to be a babysitter?" He howled, literally like the canine breeds of Wulfgor. Hopefully, he didn't ululate the galactic units while he slept like those smelly bastards. Or smell moldy like they did after a light rainfall. It took several revolutions to forget that stench.

"A nanny? You have got to be joking," she muttered.

Makl almost ducked his head in embarrassment, but an Aressotle warrior never admitted to shame. "No joke. The family requires a human female to act as a nanny for Tren's child."

"Why doesn't he take care of the thing himself?"

"He and his wife have been trying, along with others, but the child is possessed of mighty lungs and they cannot seem to make him stop using them."

"That's because babies cry."

"Aha. I shall have to let them know. See. You're helping already."

She stared at him and muttered something that sounded like "nuts" under her breath. "Sorry, purple, but that is the extent of my knowledge. I know nothing else of babies."

"Neither do they, apparently. However, having tried a variety of options, they seem to think a human female will instinctively know what to do with one."

"No way." She shook her head.

"Who said you had a choice? We made a deal."

"Well, unmake it. Ask me to do something else. You need money? I've got plenty. How about I pay you for the rescue?"

If she'd offered him sex, he might have considered it. But credits? Add to that, she crossed her arms, defiant and unbending.

Ha. He could beat her at that game. "No deal. I need a human."

"Then get another."

"No."

"Yes."

"No."

"Children," Ifruum interjected, "must we squabble right now?"

Makl's dark look went well with her growled, "Stay out of it."

"Oh, I wasn't planning to stop your little fight. As a matter of fact, I look forward to it, but I thought you'd like to postpone it to deal with the squadron of flyers coming at us now. However, if you'd rather ignore the fact they're arming their weapons to continue your little spat, then don't let me stop you."

His one ship against the miniature armada rising from the planet and its surrounding satellites? Not odds he'd take. Makl's curses matched hers for inventiveness. "This is what happens when you pair up with barbarians."

"Don't blame me for this, purple. I'm not the one leaving a trail of bodies, pissing aliens off."

"Think they'll mention it in the news?" he asked sending the ship in to a series of loops and swirls to evade the enemy's missile fire. Olivia stumbled in to the free chair and strapped in. Her fingers tapped at the console.

"Weapons system arming," announced a computerized voice.

"What are you doing?" he barked as he sent them into a sudden dive, leaving behind a ball of fire as two flyers nicked each other and exploded.

"What's it look like I'm doing? I'm going to shoot those bastards so we can escape."

To his surprise, she appeared to know her weapons system. While he armed the shields and coaxed the engine – she prepped the exterior mounted guns. Then proceeded to cackle as she took aim and fired.

After the third explosion, he couldn't resist taunting her. "Aren't you afraid you'll kill someone? I'll bet not all of those ships are manned by computers."

She didn't look up from her screen. "Space fights are different."

"Only because you can't see the carnage."

"Yup."

"Hypocrite."

"Galactic Moron."

Makl held in a grin as they bantered, especially since despite their juvenile repartee, she used the weapons with great efficiency, giving them the time needed for the engines to finish cycling. The monocle over his eye flashed coordinates and specs to star systems he could jump to. He chose a safe one that would bring them to the halfway mark and his waiting cousin. The engines reached the desired power level and they gained speed, enough to shoot off into the wide galaxy, losing their ardent pursuers.

Olivia let out a groan. "Aw. And just when I was about to beat my last high score."

She compared their escape to a video game? Did she have to be so deliciously delightful? If he'd not already found her fascinating before, her murderous quirk, which she didn't seem to realize, totally turned him on.

Danger averted, he decided it was high time he did something about it. He unbuckled and snagged the unsuspecting human before she could look up from her weapons console.

"Hey! Put me down."

"No." He settled her more firmly over his shoulder and clamped his arm over her thighs.

She pounded at his back. "I said put me down."

"That would still be a no."

"Ifruum, make him put me down," she begged her friend who watched with evident amusement.

"Nah. He's not intending to hurt you, just make you keep your word."

"But I don't want to be a nanny." Makl could hear the pout in her tone.

"Should have thought of that before."

"What do you mean?"

"He has a point. A promise is a promise."

"But he's a thief and a murderer. He probably lies all the time."

"Yes. He does. And so do you. But in some things, like when someone helps save your life, you have to keep your word. We might be hucksters, but we're not completely without honor."

Finally, the carpet said something Makl could agree with.

"You suck."

The expression Olivia used made little sense, but Makl understood the tone. She gave in with a loud sigh and let herself lie limply over his shoulder.

"I'll keep an eye for pursuit," Ifruum commented as they left.

So would Makl, remotely, while he *talked* to his cousin's new nanny – whether she wanted to or not.

*

Some friend. Ifruum threw her under the bus – a vehicle she could barely recall except for the fact it was an orangey/yellow. Earth and the life she'd led there were probably at least fifteen or more years ago. It was hard to tell with the measure of time out in space so different.

Speaking of different, nice ship. For the first time since they'd gotten on board, and left in all haste, the brief space battle an exciting video game cut short, she'd not had a chance to really note her surroundings. Now, though, holy crap. Talk about luxurious. Cream-colored walls, beige carpeting that buried the feet, and soft, hidden lighting, what a far cry from the usual vessels she traveled in. Most of the time, she and Ifruum ended up stuck on ships that dared them to take their lives in hand every time a small meteor hit.

She decided to get the conversation going. "Nice digs."

"Are you speaking of my buttocks? I perform calisthenics daily in order to stay in top form."

A giggle snuck out. She couldn't help it. Makl so loved himself. And yet, he did it in a way she couldn't help but think was cute. "Not your ass, dumdum." Even if those globes of tungsten were hot! "I meant your ship. It's really nice. Who did you steal it from?"

"What makes you think I didn't buy it? I assure you, I have the funds."

"I figured you did, what with the killing and stealing you claim to do. But, people like us don't pay for things like this." She waved her hand even if he couldn't see her, carrying her as he still was like a fleshy scarf. "So, spill."

"I met an alien who thought he was good at a certain game of chance."

"You didn't perhaps let him win a few times to enforce this belief?"

"Maybe. I was down to my last credit and a promise of a free assassination on a being of his choice when my luck turned. What do you know, I won the ship."

"How nice to hear of a gracious loser."

"Oh no. He didn't want to give it to me. Claimed I cheated. So I killed him and took it anyway. I thought it was rather generous I only took what he owed me, especially given how much I usually charge for a job. His heirs, though, didn't take it too well."

"Are you really that cold?" She reared up, for some reason wanting to see his eyes when he answered. To her surprise, he let her slide down.

"If by cold you mean emotionally detached when it comes to my work, then yes. I am a mercenary. We couldn't do our job if everything affected us."

"But the guy who owned this ship wasn't a job. You just killed him for something you wanted."

"Oh, I had other reasons, but this one is the nicest of them." He shot her an enigmatic smile. "Now, enough about me. It's time we cleared some things up about you. I am taking you to be a nanny. How long you keep that position is frankly up to you. I am just doing this as a favor to my cousin and aunt."

"A favor to your cousin and aunt? I wouldn't have thought family was important to a killer."

"Everything a warrior does is to bring glory to his name and fame to his family."

"Then why did you choose the mercenary path instead of one of honor and duty for your country?"

Makl frowned. "I don't understand your point. If the country or my home planet were attacked, I would return with due haste. All Aressotle warriors would. No one dares invade, though. We have a reputation for being merciless. So while we wait for someone stupid enough to challenge, we pursue other endeavors. I chose the mercenary route, with a few extra skills. The more dangerous the job, the more honor I bring."

"Lying and stealing aren't honorable!"

He shrugged. "In your culture, perhaps. In mine, I am just following in the footsteps of my forefathers. Besides, what do you know of honor? Did you not flout yourself as a virgin to bilk a rich patron out of his hard earned credits?"

"We both know that octopus-armed alien didn't earn that money. And I never said I had honor or integrity. I was just questioning yours. Or lack of, more specifically." She smiled.

He didn't get mad. He smiled back, way too pleased. "You do have a way of stroking a male's ego."

How did he keep doing that? Twisting her insults into compliments? How could she piss him off if he didn't react as expected? She tried to veer the topic back onto safer, more annoying ground. "So, your cousin called and asked for a nanny, and like a good boy, you fetched one. What's in it for me? Or were you all expecting me to do this for free? A girl needs things to survive."

"I have no idea, but I would assume you'll be well treated."

"Assume? Geez. Don't ever get a job as a recruiter because you suck. Do you know anything other than the fact I'm needed to help take care of a screaming brat?"

"No."

It was her turn to sigh. "You know, I'm going to quit or escape as soon as I can."

"Not my problem."

"Fine. Now, if we're done. I should go find Ifruum. I wouldn't want him to worry."

"Worry about what? He knows I won't hurt you, or kill you, though the universe knows I'd like to throttle your pale neck."

"You're not the only one thinking of throttling," she muttered. She couldn't help her gaze dropping to a spot below his waist, and damn if he didn't catch her. His knowing eyes fairly dared her to do it. To put her hands on him and...

"How long is this trip going to take?" she snapped.

"Long enough," was his reply as he tapped a spot on the wall and a door slid open.

She didn't ask long enough for what. She stomped away from him back up the hall —and cursed her disappointment when he didn't grab her and yank her close for a kiss. He'd abducted her. Shouldn't he have gotten to the ravishment part by now? Or was there a mercenary rule in that book of his against banging his cousin's new nanny?

"A fucking nanny!" She huffed the word as she flounced into the command room where Ifruum, feet propped on the console, snored. "Wake up. We need to talk, traitor."

One brown orb peered at her from under bushy brows. "I was sleeping."

"You're supposed to be on watch."

"The ship will beep if something shows up on radar."

She drummed her fingers on the armrest of the chair she flopped in. "He's an overbearing jerk."

"I take it your talk with our new friend went well."

"That man is not my friend. Or yours, for that matter. I can't believe you didn't stick up for me there."

"Even amongst thieves, we need some measure of trust. So what if he expects you to play nanny for a little while? It might be a nice change. Think of it as practice for later in life."

Have kids? She shuddered. No, thank you. The actions of her mother made it clear that having brats wasn't worth it. "I don't need practice because I am never having kids. They're too much work."

"Perhaps you'll change your mind if you meet the right person."

"Doubtful. And I didn't come to find you to talk about babies, but to find out what the plan is."

"Plan? What plan? You have a job for the next little bit."

She shot him a dirty look to go with her middle finger salute.

He laughed. "Okay. You know me too well. I have perhaps planned for a little something here and there, small side jobs, noting to interfere with you keeping your word to a certain purple dictator."

"Oh, he's a dick alright."

"Get some sleep. Relax. Take a shower. Everything will look better once you feel refreshed."

Easier said than done. While she did find a room with a small kitchen, and a bathroom for some simple cleansing, the only other rooms she located either housed ship utilities or crates, piles and piles of crates. Of all the spaces she explored, not one of them had a cot or even a couch to sleep on. A ship this luxurious had to have something more, a lounge area, crew's quarters? She just couldn't find it.

It didn't occur to her to just bunk down on a floor, soft carpeting or not. Nope, not happening, not when she knew where she'd seen a bed. A comfy-looking bed. She'd just kick a certain someone out of it. Or at least that was the excuse she gave herself that let her march with purpose to the room where she'd left Makl.

She didn't bother knocking or announcing herself, just strode in and then stopped. Gaped. Drooled a little. Possibly wet her pants. The reason? Lots of purple skin.

Fresh from a cleansing, Makl stood, naked and unashamed. Muscled, oh-so deliciously muscled and in a way even a human could appreciate – and she did – a ring pierced his left pectoral, begging for a tug. She couldn't help looking lower, at his cock, long and thick, growing as she stared… Begging her to touch. Lick. Ride.

Yeah, she wanted a piece of him. No use denying it, not when her mouth just about watered and she had to clench her fists tight lest she give in to the temptation to reach over and touch. Take. Fuck.

His lip quirked. "Human, you arrived just in time. Get naked."

"I did not come here for sex." Well, her mouth did manage to say it even if her body denied it – rather vehemently.

"Sex?" He arched a brow. "I would have thought you'd want to shower yourself first unless you are satisfied with the meager cleansing station services found off the kitchen."

She narrowed her eyes in suspicion. "You know I want to get clean. I take it you have the only full body cleansing unit on board stashed in your room."

"Through yonder opening. I'm afraid the second lavatory unit is currently inaccessible due to cargo."

"And what's the price of the shower?"

"None. Unless you think you should give me something. I am not against the whole sex thing you keep mentioning."

"I do not keep mentioning it. But we do need to talk about a bed. More specifically, my bed." Screw Ifruum who seemed capable of sleeping anywhere, upright, or even, if needed, upside down.

"Ah, yes, about the accommodations."

"Isn't there a second bedroom? I couldn't find it."

"Oh, I dare say you did, but I kind of stripped it to make room for cargo."

Damned pirate and his booty. "Well, that is going to suck for you."

"I'm sure I'll survive sharing my sleeping area. It is big, as you noticed." He winked.

She kept her eyes trained on his face and managed to not peek lower than his dimpled chin. "Yeah, that won't work. So, why don't you grab your things while I bathe? Since this is your ship, I am sure you know it well enough to find yourself a nice, comfy spot. As the only girl aboard, I declare the bed as mine." Decree made, she turned on her heel and flounced away, right into the bathroom, which held hints of moist steam.

No way. Real water? She slapped at the controls to shut and lock the door. Off came her clothes in record time and she stepped into the cubicle made to look like smooth river run rock. A moment of fiddling and the unit came on. A warm sprinkle of liquid hit her upturned face, probably not one hundred percent water, but close enough to make her close her eyes and sigh. Oh, sweet decadence.

Living in space and crowded cities had meant adapting to conservation methods still only discussed back on earth when she was abducted. Water in space was scarce, as in wars had been fought over who owned a pond-sized area of it. Planets with lots of it were wealthy. Those with none paid dearly for it.

Earth, for some reason she'd never understood, enjoyed some kind of protected status. Who enacted it or enforced it, nobody seemed to know, but other than a few small time crooks and smugglers, no one bothered with her old home and its abundant oceans.

Thinking of earth…It wasn't a place she missed much. She'd not exactly lived a perfect life there, but certain things – like showers, for instance…snow, and Snickers bars – were things you never forgot. God, she missed chocolate. Who would have thought a treat so abundant in her old life would prove so scarce in space?

She doused her head as she lamented the loss of gooey goodness and never heard him approach. When he talked, she yelped and opened streaming eyes to see him watching her.

"I thought you might like a more feminine soap." Leaning against the wall by the edge of the opaque opening, stark naked still, Makl held out the round, white bar, a half-smirk on his lips.

"I locked the door."

"A bathroom latch? Pfft. Give me some credit."

She reached out to grab the white glob, pretending it didn't affect her to have him this close. But it did affect her. All that skin and muscle… So tempting. Did the man not own clothes? Then again, it seemed a crime to cover such perfection. Unbidden, her eyes strayed lower to see him fully erect, his penis standing at attention, long, thick – and balls-free.

Dear God – who didn't exist in any galaxy she visited, no matter what Murphy's petitions stated – she'd not believed it, but he truly didn't have a sac. Or a belly button. That, more than his skin color, and teeth, made her realize the difference between them.

"How can you look so human, yet not?" she muttered. However, his strangeness didn't take away from his attractiveness. She didn't think anything could. Or so her body informed her. She was unable to stop the peaking of her nipples as she stared in fascination at his bobbing cock. Her hands rubbed slow circles on her skin. The soap lathered up nicely, making her flesh slick, which didn't help the fact she couldn't tear her gaze away from the dick that kept rising, and thickening.

"He didn't pay enough," he growled.

"Excuse me?" She didn't even pretend to understand. How could she when her hand reached between her legs, to soap herself, of course. Audience be damned. Or enjoyed.

"You are a tease."

"Who, me?" she said with a catch in her voice, rubbing her fingers across her sex with a shudder.

His eyes, hooded with a smoldering glow, stayed trained on her face. Point for him. "Do you see another human intent on driving me insane?"

"Then do something about it." She understood her challenge for what it was. Permission to seduce. Why the hell not? She wanted him. He wanted her. The sooner they got it out of their systems, the quicker he'd want to ditch her. And she could ignore him. Win. Win.

However, he didn't move, just watched. She squirmed. Her hands slowed, but didn't stop the sensual caress of her body. She flicked a glance to his cock to see it straining up, tempting her. Practically begging for her touch. For her body…

She turned from him and lifted her face to the spray. She put him from her mind. If he wanted to watch, let him. Oh God, let him watch as she cupped her breasts, lifting them into the spray, the hard, pointed tips perfect for a mouth to suck on. Sliding her hands downward, she stroked over her lean hips to the juncture of her thighs. Between them she delved, fingers finding her clit, stroking, rubbing. Enjoying herself, knowing he watched, stared, and didn't touch ignited and frustrated her.

I won't beg. No. She wouldn't. She—

Behind her, he suddenly appeared, hot and hard, pressed against her back, his hand covering hers between her legs. His lips found the lobe of her ear as he took over the caress of her pussy, his sure fingers stroking her nub. She cried out, arching into him, and he groaned, an arm wrapping around her waist, the strength of him all around her. And yet, he didn't frighten her. Overwhelmed her senses, though? Totally.

She found her cheek pressed against the smooth stone wall of the shower. The fluid still rushed warmly from the nozzles, but with his body pressed so tightly against hers, she didn't get wet, unless the spot between her thighs counted.

His cock, trapped between her legs, rubbed deliciously against the lips of her sex. And still his finger did slow circles on her clit. Fuck. She panted. She wiggled. But he didn't give her what she wanted. What they both needed.

"Why won't you ask for it?" he finally murmured in her ear as his tongue traced the shell.

She shivered. "You first."

"Ah, but I can go on for units like this. I've imagined this moment so many times. I want to savor it," he whispered. He thrust his hips against her, quick jerks that rubbed teasingly. Fingers twisted suddenly at her aching nipple. She cried out, flattening her palms against the wall. Let him torture. She wouldn't cave first, but she would come if he kept it up.

He must have sensed it. He stopped his pleasurable friction on her clit. She could have cried when he took his hand away. She throbbed fiercely. Around her body, he wrapped his own, thigh to thigh, her back to his chest, his hands over her tits. His lips latched to her neck. Dammit, a shudder rocked her. Then another. She needed him inside her so bad. Her body clenched in need, demanded she say the words.

Just when she thought she'd have to give in, he growled long and loud. "I cannot wait any longer." Back he yanked her hips, angling her lower body as he kicked apart her feet. She had just enough time to brace herself when he thrust into her.

"Oh, fuck yeah." Not the most eloquent or ladylike of epithets, but the most apt for the occasion. Never before did sex, or a cock for that matter, feel just right. Filling her up, stretching her, and doing delightful things as it weaved in and out. Her fingertips curled and scratched at the wall as her climax built and built, exploding in a wave that left her yelling, "Yes! Yes! Oh my God, yes!" And still he thrust, drawing out her bliss.

As for her second foray into pleasure? *What do you know, there is a heaven.*

*

Any other time, Makl might have taken a moment to gloat in his mastery of a female, but for the first time in his life, he lost himself in the moment. Lost himself in the pleasure. Lost himself in Olivia.

He shot his seed deep within her instead of withdrawing, understanding on a visceral level what he did, but not really caring. Something in him, something primitive, wanted her marked as his. *Mine. Mine. Mine.*

Body quaking, his hips jerked as he continued to press into her, drawing out both their climaxes. Panting, heart racing, he leaned against the shower wall and pulled her against him, cradling her limp body in his arms.

"Yeah. So…" She trailed off.

"That was certainly –" He paused, at a loss, for once, for words.

"Wickedly unexpected?"

"Very."

"Probably just pent up stress?" She sounded hopeful.

By the minor goddess Karma, he hoped so. Anything less, and anything more permanent, couldn't be entertained. Makl didn't do relationships. He'd finally gotten what he wanted. Sex with the human. It was better than he imagined. Much. The best he'd ever had – by a lot. Which made her ridiculously dangerous. The quicker he dumped her on his cousin, the better. "Mercenary rule number five, sub section five, never pass up the opportunity to empty your cock."

"How romantic." She shoved at him, a moue of annoyance on her face.

Good, that was much better. This Olivia, annoyed and scrubbing furiously so she could escape the close confines, he could handle. The one that he wanted to take in his arms to apologize, then to bed so he could sink into her, long and slow… Much too dangerous.

"So, about the whole bed sleeping thing…" She turned to glare at him, a drop of moisture hanging from the tip of her nipples almost sending him to his knees begging. "I'm sleeping in it."

"So am I."

"Can't you go somewhere else?" she groused.

"It's the only bed. And if you think I'm sleeping on the floor of my own ship…"

"Fine. We can share it, but you keep to your side. Since you've taken care of your mercenary rule concerning your cock, I better not have to worry about you bugging me."

Hmm, should he mention he could go again in about...oh, look at that. He was ready to go now. Better hide that before she took the bed away. Lucky him, she turned and bent over, giving him an enticing view.

"Are you looking for something?" Because if she wanted, he could hide his dick in her sex and wait for her to find it.

"Where have you hidden your clothes? And why is it so neat in here? It's unnatural. Men are natural born slobs."

"Slovenliness is not tolerated. Unless as part of a subterfuge to hide our identity," he repeated by rote. The ability to move and wipe his presence was important to one of his ilk. Besides, he hated clutter.

"Well, just so you know, I'm a slob."

Good. It would help negate some of her appeal. He needed something, anything to prevent him from lusting after her like a warrior in his first stages of sexual experimentation. Did she release a pheromone of some sort, something exclusive to humans that made her so frukxing irresistible?

He lay upon his mattress and hid his hard state, watching her with hooded eyes. She found a shirt, put it on so that it hung around her knees, and paced in it. He should have ignored her and slept, but fascination kept him watching her.

"What has you agitated now?" he finally asked.

"Nothing."

"Then turn off the lights and come to bed. You are distracting me from my slumber time."

"Does my purple killer need his beauty rest?"

"Yes. Dealing with a cranky, stubborn barbarian is tiring." He closed his eyes on her stunned expression, his lips curved in satisfaction. They opened on his forceful exhalation as she landed on his chest with a growled, "I'm tiring?"

He peered up at her, her wet hair spiked, her eyes flashing with annoyance, her lips full and tempting. A moment later, he pinned her to her back, latched his mouth to hers, and slid into her, all in one fell swoop.

"Oh. I thought we'd agreed this was a onetime thing?" she huffed as her fingers dug into his shoulders.

"It's been awhile since I exercised my cock," he grunted, the act of coherent speech almost beyond him as her slick channel suctioned at him.

"One last time then. No more after this," she panted. "I don't even like you."

"Me either. Last time. I swear." He lied. Somehow, he doubted he'd come close to assuaging his desire for her, something he promptly forgot as all the blood in his brain left to aid his cock in finding mental clarity.

They both came in a frantic, panting climax that left him limp. Sated, for some reason, he didn't roll over and ignore her– or toss her from his bed – but under the guise of keeping her close lest she try something devious, settled her into the cradle of his arms where they both fell asleep, cuddling.

Chapter Seven

Makl woke first, and held his breath as he realized what the warm bundle of skin snuggled against his body meant.

I slept with a female! Not just slept, but spooned and held intimately. He'd shared his bed, pillow, and blanket with someone else. The horror of it spurred him to action. So quickly she never felt him move, he escaped the bed and left Olivia slumbering in the warm spot his body left behind.

Heart racing, he eyed her and wondered what came over him. The previous night, he'd meant to seduce her, lull her to sleep, then place her on the pallet currently folded into the wall. Instead, relaxed, if still somewhat horny despite the two rounds, he fell asleep, cradling the human's delectable body. *I snuggled!* The galactic avenger, seducer of females, disruptor of rapturous unions, did not snuggle. Or let his guard down – especially to sleep alongside a human who'd proven herself devious in the past, and whose partner currently manned the ship.

Someone else drove his ship? Dammit. Just how much had this barbarian addled his wits? He'd have to pay closer attention in the future to make sure he kept some blood in his brain. Mistakes like this could cost a mercenary his life.

Dressing quicker than the time that husband came home early from work – only an idiot would confront an eight foot Gorrolian with razor sharp tusks – he fled his room – without taking a last tempting glance at the barbarian in his bed – and made his way to the control chamber. He didn't know what he expected to find, but he feared the answer. A million possibilities came to mind, all of them sure to make him the cause of derision at the next family reunion. Unless, he regained control, killed everyone on board so there were no witnesses, and then accomplished some spectacular, dangerous act. He might still be able to save the situation unless Olivia's talking pet did something completely unexpected. The furry face, shaggy ears, and overall benign appearance didn't fool him. For all he knew, the shaggy rug sat in his chair, yipping as he drove them into the nearest sun. *Now you're being ridiculous, of course. Why ruin a perfectly good ship when he could kill me or have me killed?* Maybe that was why Olivia came to his room and seduced him. But, he foiled her murderous intent by sexing her so thoroughly she needed to rest and recuperate. The Galactic Lover struck again.

Ooh, he'd have to remember that line.

First, though, he'd regain control of his ship – and himself. However, once again, a little thing known as Murphy's Law, which had a section devoted to it in his mercenary handbook, proved that when you thought perhaps you'd gotten a handle on things, Murphy, the god he refused to believe in, did something to frukx things up, forcing a warrior to think fast on his feet. In his case, he walked into the command center and didn't find a walking carpet, but a very human male sipping from an oddly-shaped cup with a small plate underneath it.

Long-haired, wearing a flaring navy blue coat over a white linen shirt, adorned in effeminate ruffles, the strange male cocked an amused brow at Makl's appearance.

"Did you have a nice *rest?*" the intruder asked.

"Who the frukx are you?" snarled Makl, fingers flexing, reaching for the knife at his back. Like he'd go anywhere without a weapon.

"Oh, you know me, just not usually in this guise. Some call me that whoreson. Others, god. One certain pupil of mine is fond of Ifruum, but myself, I prefer my more worshipped name of Murphy. As in the god, Murphy."

"Gods don't exist." Except for Karma, of course, but it took some work on her part to convince him.

"You say I don't exist and yet, here I am."

Yes, there he was. "So you hid onboard beforehand. Damned stowaway." Makl didn't miss the male's teeth grinding together. Ah, the sweet sound of annoyance.

"You and I both know that's not the case. There was nobody onboard. You had the ship run a diagnostic while you played hide your wick with the girl."

"How did you know that?" Makl thought furiously as he tried to figure out an explanation. A quick look around showed the ship still in hyper mode, and he would have felt a slowdown, post coital nap or not. "Who are you really and how did you get on my ship? And what did you do with Olivia's companion? The walking rug?"

Before Makl's disbelieving eyes, the male shimmered and turned in to a shaggy mess. "You mean my alter ego Ifruum? He's still here. But, I find his shape rather restrictive and smelly." The rug morphed back into a man. "I take it you believe me now?"

"Impossible." Makl thought shape-shifters a sham. He'd even wagered about it once. Frukx it all, now he owed his bloody cousin a bottle of that expensive wine he liked so much.

"How can you say impossible when you saw it with your own two eyes?"

"Damn you. You just cost me a bottle of expensive wine, wine I had plans for."

"Get over it."

"Does Olivia know?" Makl asked, as he lowered himself into his seat and casually took a closer look at the ship readings.

"Does the girl know that her uncle Murphy is also her beloved mentor? No. She's the reason I had to become that stupid walking dog in the first place. Get into a few misunderstandings, add in the teenage years, and suddenly, the kid doesn't listen anymore to the uncle who saved her. I was tired of replacing the dishes she kept throwing at my head, so I left, but she was too young and naïve to survive on her own. So being a benevolent god, I threw on a dog suit with big puppy eyes, gave her the promise of money, and suddenly, she's Miss Agreeable."

Makl reeled from the information, processing it and how it affected him. It didn't. "So why tell me? Aren't you afraid I'll let her know?" Makl wondered what he could soak the shape-shifter for to keep silent. Mercenary rule number seven: if a blackmail opportunity arises, use it to make some credits.

"Alas, I fear the time for my charade grows to a close. Soon, Olivia won't need me to protect and guide her anymore."

"You'd leave that female to fend for herself?" Having touched her, Makl could attest to her fragile nature. She wouldn't survive on her own without a strong male to protect her. *A male like me.* Not that he planned to volunteer.

"Leave her? Not exactly, but even I can't stop her destiny, a destiny she'll have to be dragged into, probably kicking and screaming."

Before Makl could question Murphy – or at least the shape-shifting imposter posing as the mischievous entity – Olivia sauntered in wearing one of Makl's shirts, and a pair of his pants, the cuffs rolled a few times. She looked adorable. Instantly, his cock filled, but on guard for it, Makl pinched himself hard, using the pain to keep his lust from stealing any more blood from his brain. He intended to keep his wits about him from here on out.

"What are you doing here?" she snapped, her eyes flashing with annoyance.

At first, Makl thought she yelled at him, but her stabbing finger waved at another source.

"Olivia, my dear niece." The intruder used a placating tone, and Makl shook his head. Even he knew better than to do that with an irate female.

"Don't you *niece* me. I disowned you."

"But we're family."

"By adoption only. Thank God."

"You're welcome."

"Not you. You're not a god. More like a pain in my –" She finally deigned to notice they had an audience and her cheeks turned pink. Not as pink as they'd flushed last night, though, when he'd…

Whack. He shot his fist sideways and let his knuckles connect with the metal post running from floor to ceiling. The sudden pain put his dirty thoughts away, leaving him clear-headed. Makl waggled the fingers on his other hand at her. "Hello, barbarian."

"Purple. You're looking rather frazzled today." She smirked at his unkempt appearance.

Ignoring her attempt to get a rise out of him, he fired back, "Well it's hard to look my best when someone interrupted my period of rest with mighty snoring. I never thought a female could make such a ruckus."

"I do not."

"Oh, you do," he said, echoed by Murphy.

"Jerks," she muttered. "Where's Ifruum? What did you do to him this time, Murphy?"

"Me? Why must you always blame me? I'm just the man who always had your best interest at heart. Who saved you from a life of servitude and –"

"Blah. Blah. Blah. Yes, you're just a hero. I know. You and Makl should start a club for aliens with big egos who feel underappreciated."

"Hey, who doesn't appreciate me?" Makl protested. "And why do I have to share the club? It should be all about me."

"I was just going to say the same thing," Murphy exclaimed.

"Oh my God, you're just like twins. Barf. Now that we've ascertained you're perfect for each other, can someone tell me what's going on? Murphy, what are you doing here? Purple, where's my breakfast? And would someone tell Ifruum to stop napping wherever he is and get his furry ass here?"

Makl leaned sideways and whispered, "Is she always this demanding?"

"Yes."

"I heard that. And I'm still waiting."

She was, too – foot tapping, arms crossed. She actually expected them to obey. Makl snickered. "She's insane."

"Yes. But I'm fond of her in spite of it," Murphy said on a sigh.

"Well, since you're both just a fountain of information, I'm leaving. Bye, Murph. Hope you get stuck on that comet again and go for a ride."

Out flounced the human, leaving Makl gaping. "How did I ever believe she was a demure virgin?"

"The girl is a born actress. It's why she's so good at what she does."

"How did you come across her?"

"You could say I accidentally rescued her. But that's not my story to tell. Suffice it to say, I made the mistake of keeping her and she's been making me pay for it ever since." Murphy said it as if it annoyed him, but his tone and expression told a different story. The shape-shifter cared for the female.

Makl decided not to kill her uncle – yet. "Isn't she going to get suspicious when she doesn't find her furry friend?"

"Who says she isn't?"

"You're sitting in front of me, so unless you can be in two places at once, I'm pretty sure she'll notice."

Murphy's smile widened.

"Are you implying you can be in two places at once?" The possibilities boggled his mind.

"And before you ask, it's a god-given gift, not a gadget."

Damn. Makl slid his knife back in his sheath. "So what is your plan?"

"What plan? I thought we were dropping Olivia off to become a nanny?"

"We are. But that plan doesn't include you."

"Oh don't worry about me. Once my girl is safe and sound, I'll pop off somewhere new for a spot of fun. There're always people praying to me. It's just a matter of choosing who will get my divine attention."

A snort escaped him. "I see where the craziness comes from."

"I wouldn't talk. Your family isn't exactly known for its sane decisions."

"Why thank you. We take great pride in distinguishing ourselves from the others."

"In that respect, you've done well. But…"

"But what?"

Murphy's cup and plate disappeared into thin air as he leaned back, suddenly sitting in a plush, gold fabric-covered seat. He steepled his fingers. "Well, we are still quite a few days out from your cousin's, and with some of your funds temporarily frozen –"

"Frozen!"

"Yes, the Obsidian Galaxy filed a formal complaint and had an injunction placed on your credit accounts. Don't worry, that councilor in your family, what's his name again?"

"Tren," Makl supplied through gritted teeth.

Murphy snapped his fingers. "Ah yes, Tren, is already arranging to have the injunction removed, but in the meantime, I thought you might like bit of adventure and liquid currency."

"What kind of adventure?"

"A jewelry store heist. I planned it as soon as the owner started boasting his security was foolproof."

Oh, those magical, challenging words. Makl leaned forward, more eager than he wanted to admit. "Tell me more."

"It seems he's installed a state of the art system comprised of cameras, scanners, and guards. He also runs background checks on all of his clients."

"Sounds tight. What's the payoff?"

"A ring with a priceless stone."

"Nice, but not worth the time I'd have to waste planning. The family is expecting me. Perhaps on my way back from dropping Olivia off."

"What planning? I've already got it all figured out. I'd initially planned to play the part of doting fiancé myself, but given Olivia won't work with me but only that stupid dog, I don't know how believable we'd be. But if you were to act the part of loving fool who's proposed, why, I think it would work perfectly."

"You want me to steal it with her as my partner? Are you out of our frukxing mind? I work alone." Yet, at the same time, he couldn't deny the intrigue of having her by his side while they pulled off a heist.

"Can you imagine the headlines? *Galactic Avenger and his lovely assistant steal priceless ring.*"

Makl could see it. And frukx if he didn't like it. A moment later, he'd agreed and they hammered out the details.

*

Olivia stomped off in search of food and her partner in crime. Seeing her uncle Murphy again after all this time threw her for a loop, but not as much as facing the guy who'd wormed his way under her defenses the night before. The purple pompous idiot not only seduced her, but somehow got her to fall asleep in his arms.

Talk about letting down her guard in a major way. But worse than knowing she left herself vulnerable to a male she barely knew – a male she enjoyably, if rashly, had sex with – she hated how the first thing that happened when she woke, alone, was her feeling of disappointment.

She should have reveled in the fact he didn't attempt round three, a seduction she would have rejected – probably. She'd scratched her itch, which should tide her over for oh, the next few years of her life.

Olivia wasn't a virgin, but neither did she possess a high sex drive. She rarely felt the urge for something carnal. When she did, she scratched it with either a compatible entity or her own hand. The itch went away and she went on with her life.

So why was it that seeing Makl again brought all the same feelings and attraction right back? And not just back, but times a hundred. Now, when she looked at his strong, capable hands, she didn't just imagine what they would feel like on her body, she knew. She craved them. She wanted those hands touching her body and those lips nibbling her skin. She wanted to taste the ecstasy he showed her. Damn his purple hot bod, she wanted him – again.

How annoying. Confused, annoyed, and hornier than she liked, she left Makl conversing with

Murphy – which surely didn't bode well – and went in search of something to fill her belly.

Into the small food prep area she stomped, finding Ifruum scrounging through the cupboards. His familiar puppy dog eyes swung her way.

"What's got you scowling?"

"Did you know Murphy was here?"

"Yes. He was worried about you. Apparently, he saw your picture on the new feeds and got concerned. Congratulations. It seems you're a wanted lady."

"I am?"

"Yes, you are. A tape of your shenanigans with the purple mercenary from your temporary jail cell has been circulating. You wouldn't believe the monetary offers being bandied for a full, unedited version."

The words emerged from her automatically. "How much? Wait a second." She slapped her forehead. "What am I saying? I am not doing a sex tape."

"Why not? Did you not have sex with the mercenary?"

"Yes. And? It's not like it meant anything. Just a couple of compatible bodies exercising a natural need."

"Going to keep exercising it for the whole trip?"

"Of course not." Um, maybe one more time, just to get him out of her system. Stupid, scruffy-looking man. No one should look that delicious with his hair standing on end, his shirt half tucked, and jaw unshaven. Makl did, and suddenly, just once—even twice—wasn't enough.

"Keep in mind, I don't care if you do or not, just don't it anywhere I can see it or you'll be cleaning up the puke." Ifruum shuddered.

"I think I can restrain myself," she replied dryly, not at all amused.

"Good, because I want you concentrating on our next job."

Ah yes, her partner in crime and his *jobs*. Where he got his ideas from, Olivia didn't know, but Ifruum always had a lead on a scam. Most of the time, it ended in profit, even with the various disasters with which they usually had to contend. They had more than their fair share, probably her adopted parentage to Murphy rubbing off. As she listened to his latest proposal while wondering what Makl and Murphy talked about, she had only one thing to say at the end of Ifruum's spiel.

"I don't like it."

"What part of the plan don't you like?" Ifruum asked, bushy brows beetled as he handed her a steaming cup of something that passed for coffee in space. Not that she had any experience with the real stuff. Young and poor when she was abducted, she was lucky if she got something other than water to drink at home.

"I like the plan just fine. And while I think Makl is a pompous idiot who loves himself, I agree he'd make a better fiancé than you. What I don't like is the fact Murphy popped in for a visit."

"Don't be so hard on him. You know he loves you in his own fashion."

Yeah, but his fashion tended to cause things around him to self-destruct, which in turn meant things around her also went to hell when he decided to put in an appearance. "I know he does. And I am so grateful to him for what he's done, but come on, even you have to admit, having him around means everything that can go wrong, will. I have a hard enough time escaping his influence when he doesn't visit. I can just imagine what will happen now that he has."

"But at least it makes things more exciting."

"And dangerous. Have you forgotten that part?"

"We always survive."

"For how long?" she grumbled.

Ifruum handed her a plate of food – the lumps never resembled anything she remembered of food as a child. What she wouldn't give to one day get a hold of a cheeseburger, an honest to God, McDonald's cheeseburger and fries. It was the one memory she clung to tenaciously, the one thing she could remember as being the sum of everything that tasted yummy in the world – until Makl that was. Damn, but the man made her drool, and here she was planning to act the part of his lovesick fiancée.

"I won't have to kiss him or something, will I?" *Please say yes.*

"Depends on if the shop owner gets suspicious."

"How long until we reach the new job?"

"An earth day, give or take a few hours."

Too much time. She sighed. "I guess I should go see if Uncle Murphy has left and if Makl survived his interrogation."

Ifruum chuffed. "What makes you think Murphy is grilling him?"

"Makl slept with his favorite *niece*." She air quoted. "He'll be lucky if he survives the day without a mishap."

Ifruum stayed behind to clean up as she headed to the command room. How would Makl act? Hell, how would she? She'd never fallen asleep with a man before. She'd also never wanted a man for round two, let alone a round three. Would he act as if nothing happened or changed? Or would he expect something more of her? He wouldn't suddenly become clingy, would he? She didn't think she could abide a clingy man.

Sweeping into the room, she almost sighed with relief when she noted her uncle had vacated the premises. At least that problem was temporarily gone, again leaving her with one delicious looking alien who lounged in his seat while…what was he doing?

She turned to look at the screen holding his attention and gasped. "Is that supposed to be us?"

"Yes. We're famous." While grainy – the prison budget not allowing for more expensive cameras – the image certainly didn't lie. There she was, in living color, kissing Makl and talking nonsense.

"This is the video of our jailbreak."

"Yes. Apparently it's quite the sensation."

"Sensational piece of drivel." She wrinkled her nose. "Oh God, I can't believe people are listening to that crap."

"Listening, loving, and begging for an encore, but this time with less clothes."

"Not happening."

"Why not?" Makl grinned and waved his hand. "Don't you want to be famous?"

"Famous for doing porn? No thank you."

"Does the why of it really matter?"

"Yes, it does."

"Females. So irrational."

"Men, always thinking with their penises," she sassed back.

He threw his head back and laughed. "You are funny, barbarian."

"And you have a warped sense of humor. Can you turn that shit off now? I can't listen to it anymore." Because who wanted to listen when she wanted to live it? "What did my uncle have to say for himself?"

"Not much. He just wanted to introduce himself."

"And did he threaten you with his brand of curse if you sullied me? Demand you treat me right or else?"

"No. Was he supposed to? I actually kind of liked the fellow, which I'll admit surprised me given what I know of him."

Murphy hadn't bullied Makl into promising to stay away? That didn't bode well. Murphy acting devious meant all kinds of trouble. She'd have to keep her eyes open lest Makl inadvertently succumb to the smothering protection of the deity who'd chosen to adopt her.

"Don't get too complacent. Murphy never does anything without a reason."

"Or he likes me." Her purple mercenary winked.

God forbid. "Don't ever wish that on anyone," she said with a shudder. "I speak as someone who knows."

"Why didn't you tell me you were adopted by an entity who thinks he's a god?"

"Because I've been trying to forget," she muttered.

"It must have made life interesting growing up?"

"Interesting if you don't mind having chaos constantly erupting around you. I learned from an early age to expect the unexpected. Like at my graduation from the Guild of Pick Pocketing, a normal uncle would have arranged for fireworks. That wasn't good enough apparently. The third sun in the star system exploded into a thousand meteoric bits forcing a sudden planet wide evacuation. And you don't even want to know what happened to the first boy I kissed."

Makl leaned forward not at all put off. "Actually, I do want to know. Did he eviscerate him? Cut off his head?"

"Nothing that blood thirsty. Nope, the poor guy developed a rare allergy to human saliva and almost choked to death. But that's nothing compared to the first boy who dumped me." She shuddered in recollection. "Let's just say, Karma took care of that problem when ice cream didn't do the trick."

"Karma as in the goddess?" he queried with lifted brows.

"The one and only. You've heard of her?"

"To my misfortune. I happen to be one of her followers."

She couldn't help but chuckle. "Sucker! Enough, though, of my aunt and uncle. I hear you're going to help Ifruum and I pull off a heist. Have you done this kind of scam before?"

"Child's play. Just put yourself in my hands, which as you recall, are quite capable, and together, we can overcome any burden."

That's what I'm afraid of.

Chapter Eight

They spent most of the day going over their plans for the heist. Working with a team would prove interesting. Makl usually performed alone, but he couldn't deny he wanted to do this, in spite of the delay to the errand for his aunt. The idea of spending more time with Olivia should have set off warning alarms; instead, he enjoyed every jibe she threw his way, every smirk she bestowed, each heated glance when she thought him not paying attention.

It seemed he wasn't the only one who couldn't forget the explosive sex of the previous day. He also wasn't the only one fighting not to succumb again, a fight he knew they'd lose by the way the air fairly sizzled around them.

At the end of the day, as fatigue claimed her, or so he judged by her yawns, he broached it. "It occurs to me –"

"Hold the presses, purple has an idea."

"You know, if your tongue feels such a need to exercise then I have something you can use it on." He grabbed his crotch and waggled it at her.

She made a face. "Eeew! Oh, how gross."

Offended, he blurted the first thing that came to mind. "That's not what you thought yesterday."

"That was then. This is now. I had an urge, you were handy. I'm good now so you can stop trying to get into my pants. It isn't happening again."

"Really?"

"Yes, really. Despite what you think, you're not irresistible. You scratched your itch. I scratched mine. It was okay. Kind of quick, though, to tell the truth. Now, if you'll excuse me, I want to get some sleep. Alone."

Off she strode to his room, buttocks wiggling, without a backwards glance. But she'd made one fatal mistake. She'd insulted and challenged him, thus invoking two mercenary rules. He couldn't let this go unanswered. He stalked after her, entering his room just moments after her. She whirled to face him and held up a hand.

"Stop right there, purple. I meant what I said about sleeping alone."

"It's my bed. If you don't like it, then you can find other accommodations."

"I'm your guest, which means I get dibs."

"No, we're currently partners, which means what's mine is mine."

"That makes no sense."

"It doesn't have to. I'm sleeping in this bed. Right now. Whether you choose to join me or not, is up to you."

"So you'd relegate me to the floor? That's not very gentlemanly."

"Who ever said I was gentle?"

She scowled. "Fine. We'll share. But no funny business."

"I didn't hear you laughing last time we were in it attending to *business*. As I recall, you spent that time trying to catch your breath and relegating me to deity status, or so your yelling indicated at the time."

"You are unbelievably arrogant."

"It isn't arrogant to be truthful. I gave you great pleasure."

"So what, I didn't contribute?"

He pretended to think about it, tapping his chin. "Actually, other than spreading your thighs and screaming, not really. I did all the work."

Her mouth gaped open. "You son of a bitch. You just called me a bad lay. I should kill you."

"Please try. I'd enjoy a bit of foreplay before we have sex again." He raised a brow in mockery.

"We are not having sex."

"I'd like to wager on that. I love a sure win." His smile was probably a tad too smug, which meant he deserved the fist to this stomach, but the knee to his groin? Totally uncalled for.

"I hate you."

Yeah, he kind of got that given the pain still radiating from his male parts. As if he'd reward her now with his sexual expertise. Let her suffer. "Good. I'd hate for you to lament my loss when we part ways. Despise me all you want. Loathe me, actually, if you can. I hear angry sex is the best kind."

"Hope you and your hand have a good time then," she sassed. She proceeded to ignore him, whirling on her heel to march away. She went to the lavatory.

Saucy barbarian. He clued in on the invitation right away. Stripping, he approached the door, not surprised to find it locked. She couldn't give in too easily. He entered the code to open it. It didn't work. He used his override.

Access Denied.

Excuse me? Perhaps he entered it wrong. Makl tapped in the master override code, the one that unlocked any frukxing door on the ship.

Access Denied.

He queried the computer logs and cursed under his breath as he saw the trail of perfidy she created. The human had outsmarted him. Somehow, she'd managed to create a new master key and relegated his to secondary status.

I am going to kill her. Where's my pistol? He'd shoot the lock off the door and strangle her pale neck. No, if he touched her naked, wet body, he might forget himself and his cock would use that time to take over. Better if he killed her right away. Shot her dead. But then she'd make a mess in his shower. The only shower. Nope, he'd have to brave the glistening wet skin and toss her luscious body out into space. Or he could…

…get even. She wanted to deny her attraction to him. Pretend she didn't want him. Ha. He knew better. And he'd prove it. She wasn't the only one who could play games.

"Well played, barbarian. Very well played," he muttered. "But, this is not over. Not by a long stretch." She might think herself one step ahead of him now, but Makl would prevail in the end – and have her begging.

When she emerged awhile later, dewy-skinned and clean, already naked – if wrapped in a towel – he made sure to pat her on the buttocks and lift her chin to close her mouth as he sauntered past, nude and ready to bathe. He left the door open so the steam could billow out, knowing she surely imagined his wondrous naked body under the hot spray, remembered the feel of their bodies joined together the previous day as the warm liquid cascaded over their forms.

He knew he couldn't forget it. He replayed that wondrous moment with her as he cleansed himself. But he did nothing to ease his discomfort. Not yet. Wrapping just a towel around his shoulders and nothing else, his cock too engorged to hide, he expected to see her eagerly waiting, ready to beg for his touch. Instead, soft snores met him.

She'd gone to sleep!

Consternation must have surely marked his expression as he stood over her slumbering form. How could she sleep at a time like this? He was horny. She was horny. He knew she was. Unless…She wouldn't have dared.

He leaned down and sniffed her hands. The distinct musk of her sex coated her fingers. The barbarian had pleasured herself instead of using him! How dare she take care of her arousal without waiting for him? *She cheated.* This meant war.

Rational or not, Makl couldn't help but plot ways to get her to succumb to her lust for him, because he'd be damned if he'd let a horny female satisfy herself on his ship when he had a perfectly good tongue and cock at her disposal. Before this voyage ended, he'd have her begging for him or his name wasn't the Galactic Conqueror. Now *there* was a name that screamed success.

*

Oh yes. That felt good. Olivia gasped and the coiling heat increased. Her pleasure mounted. Her hips thrust against the mouth latched to her clit. A moan slipped out. Her eyes fluttered open as she woke to a thorough tonguing of her pussy.

It occurred to her she should protest Makl's assault on her girly parts. And she would, right after she came on his tongue. Seriously, the man knew his way around down there. Back and forth he lapped across her swollen nub. Forget the workout she'd given it with her fingers the night before. The small orgasm she achieved – as she imagined him in the shower – wouldn't even come close to the climax she felt building.

"Oh God, yes," she moaned. "Don't stop. I'm going to come." She reached down and grabbed his hair only to feel him slip away. Her poor pussy noted the travesty first, cooling without his breath and mouth to keep it warm. She twitched her hips, but the pleasure didn't return. Makl climbed off the bed from between her thighs and stretched all six-foot-plus naked inches of mauve hotness. A rush of heat kept her arousal high. God, he truly was a work of art. Staring at him proved a decadence all to itself. Even his ass was hot, super hot and walking away?

What. The. Fuck. "Where are you going?" she managed to croak, as her clit continued to throb, waiting for the grand finale.

"You're awake."

"What does that have to do with you stopping what you were doing?"

"We're almost at our destination. Since you were sleeping and I wasn't sure how to wake you, I did so in a way I knew I'd personally enjoy. So make note of it for future reference."

Fine. She got the hint. "Aren't you forgetting something?" she asked, wiggling her hips in reminder.

Striding away once again, taut buttocks flexing, he stopped and snapped his fingers. "Yes. As a matter of fact, I am."

Olivia settled herself in and waited for him to continue his oral version of an alarm clock.

"Ifruum says your breakfast is ready whenever your lazy ass is." And with that, Makl closeted himself in the bathroom.

He did not just leave.

He did. Unbelievable. She stared at the door, then down at her denuded, flushed, and very aroused body. That fucking jerk. She didn't know what game he played this time, but as usual, she didn't care for it. Nor did she have time to take care of it because a speaker crackled to life.

"Olivia! I know you can't still be sleeping. Get a move on, girl. We're almost there."

Yeah, I almost was. Maybe she could...

Makl emerged, still naked, and she flopped over on the bed, face first. She groaned into the pillow. Then yelled as he sneaked up on her to murmur in her ear, "Ask me nicely and maybe I'll give you what you apparently don't need."

"When hell freezes over."

"Considering that galaxy has never thawed, that makes no sense."

"Just go away."

"I'd rather stay and watch. I know you touched yourself thinking of me, barbarian. I find it incredibly arousing. I can't wait to see you do it in person. Perhaps I will touch myself, too. We can masturbate together."

For a moment, his words almost tempted her into doing it. Her body throbbed so fiercely. But then, that meant he would win. She'd lose her upper hand. She'd...

Screw it. She rolled onto her back before she dragged his head down and mashed her mouth against his. "Just shut up and fuck me already, would you? My breakfast is getting cold."

He didn't need to be told twice. He broke off the kiss, but before she could protest, his heavy body settled atop hers, upside down. Forget a hard fuck. He was going back for seconds.

She gasped as his tongue found her clit, a sound cut off as the tip of him, engorged and tasting sweet, slipped into her mouth. Not very experienced in this type of sexual play didn't mean she didn't grasp the concept. Up and down his length she licked, sliding her tongue over silken skin. She tongued the tip of him. She took him into her mouth and sucked. Despite having never participated in oral sex before, she caught on quick. She simply did to his cock whatever came to mind, and damn if he didn't get thicker, his movements more frantic.

It became harder to concentrate and breathe as his mouth wreaked sexual havoc on her pussy. Several times, her hips bowed off the bed and each time he slowed down, leaving her on the edge, panting. When he slid a few of his fingers into her as he plied her clit with his tongue?

She screamed around his cock and clamped down, sucking as hard as she could, hips bucking. His whole body went still except for his fingers and mouth. His cock pulsed, then throbbed again before coming in a hot gush. She lost her tight latch and did her best to take his pleasure just as he continued to draw hers out until she fairly sobbed.

Spent and panting, she couldn't even open her eyes when he carefully extricated himself from the bed. But she didn't lack the energy needed to flash him a rude gesture when he smugly said, "Well, I don't know about you, but I know I feel much more clear-headed now."

Chapter Nine

〰〰〰〰〰〰〰〰〰〰〰〰〰〰〰〰〰〰〰〰〰〰〰〰

Makl could feel her sitting tensely at his side as the luxurious aircar he'd ordered upon their arrival at the small trading planet coasted them to their destination. "Relax."

"I am." Olivia's reply emerged as stiff as her coiffure, a wigged concoction she'd somehow conjured from out of his many storage crates.

"No, you're not."

"Fine then. I'm not. Give me a break. I'm going over the plan in my mind, trying to make sure we haven't missed anything."

Eyeing her – cool and regal with her straight back and primly folded hands, the only outward display of her nerves was a luscious lower lip tucked between teeth – Makl shook his head. "Oh, you missed something alright."

She met his gaze with a questioning one. "I did? What?"

He reached out to touch her and she automatically leaned away. "That is what's wrong. We're supposed to be a couple besotted with each other. We'd have to be if I am crazy enough to want to give you a ring of such value, but there you are, acting like a frigid virgin, which we both know you aren't."

"Never going to let me live that down, are you?"

"No."

"Okay, so we're not a lovey-dovey couple. Big deal. Not everyone buying a ring is all over each other smooching and groping."

"Says a female who obviously has much to learn. Trust me when I say we don't look anything like a couple shopping for something romantic. In order for us to pull this off, we need to make this believable."

"What do you propose?" she questioned.

"I need you to look at me like you want to strip me naked and lick me." Seriously, he did. And then, if she wanted to act upon her thoughts, he wouldn't say no.

"That's just perverted."

"You didn't think that this morning."

A pink stain colored her pale cheeks. "A momentary aberration."

He snorted. "You are such a bad liar."

"Fine. I enjoyed it. I don't need to recapture that moment, though, to make some merchant think we're in love."

"I beg to differ. What is love but another word for lust? Lust with a touch of something more. Something hot. Passionate." Ah, there was the flicker of heat he wanted. Olivia licked her lips, a slow, sensual swipe of her tongue that took him from semi-erect to rock hard. "Now I realize we can't fake the love, but we sure know all about the lust." Love was for weaklings. Unlike his cousins, Makl would never fall for it. Never let a female dictate to –

Ooh, there was the look he wanted. *All for me.* The possessive thought didn't distract him, not in the face of the languorous heat that invaded Olivia's gaze, a heat he now knew all too well...and craved. Their eyes locked. She took in a sharp breath. He leaned forward, she didn't move, but her lashes fluttered, shuttering her mesmerizing eyes.

She might hide the doorway to her innermost thoughts, but she couldn't hide the hardness of her nipples poking through the tight silk of her top. "I thought you took care of my lust? Or have you forgotten I came? I'm afraid I'm all lusted out. Sorry."

He expected the challenge, something he noticed she enjoyed doing, but instead of replying, he pulled Olivia onto his lap. Her ornate gown – pulled from one of his crates of stolen goods – might cover her down to her trim ankles encased in soft malleable boots, but he knew the fabric did nothing to hide the erection pressing under her buttocks. Her breathing grew shallow and uneven, a signal of her arousal, or so he'd noticed on previous occasions. He thumbed her lower lip until she parted it from the top with a sigh. How he enjoyed her small sounds of pleasure. He leaned forward and traced the line of her mouth, inhaling her warm breath, tasting the sweetness of the makeup balm making her lips shine. She didn't pull away – on the contrary, she angled closer, her hungry mouth searching for his.

Yanking on the loose fabric of her skirt, he slid his hands up her thighs, reveling in the silken softness of her skin, the way she heated for him and her heart rate sped up. He didn't stop his ascent until he reached her ribs. Unfettered, her breasts were a welcome weight in his palms and he thrummed her nipples, his mouth salivating for a taste. But he managed to retain enough sense to know he didn't have time for that. He nibbled her lower lip instead, sucking it then switching to her top one until she clung at him, her fingers tugging at the hair curling over the nape of his neck. Sideways she turned onto his lap, the skirt of her dress riding up over her hips as she straddled him, rocking her core against the bulge in his pants, driving them both wild with need.

Careful not to ruin her stylish coiffure, he gripped the back of her neck, and angled her just right. She opened her mouth for his kiss, no longer protesting, rather panting and moaning, her earlier arguments lost amidst her rising passion. In slid his tongue to duel with hers, a sensual glide that drew forth a moan from her. She squirmed in his lap. What torture, especially since the car door was flung open in that moment. It took him only a nanosecond longer than he liked to tuck her into his side, pull out his hidden gun, and have it aimed at the face peering within. A dozen faceted eyes blinked as the three mouths, painted orange, blue, and green, rounded into an O of surprise.

"Ahem. Sorry for the interruption," the alien stuttered.

Not as sorry as I am. He should have asked for the scenic route. Makl cradled Olivia's frame, her muscles already rigid again as she prepared to enact their plan.

Time for the act to begin.

"You should count yourself lucky I'm feeling benevolent, or you'd be dead." Makl took his time lowering his gun.

Olivia fluttered her lashes and gasped. "He doesn't mean that."

Um, yeah he did. On a job or not, Makl didn't like rudeness, and interrupting him with Olivia now rated high on his list of things not to do.

Olivia gushed on. "It's just… he's so possessive and passionate. It's a good thing he's planning to marry me, because I don't know how much longer I can hold myself back." She pressed her hand to her chest and batted her eyelids.

A trifle much, but Makl liked her style. *This is going to be fun.*

"You have my apologies, sir. Ma'am." The head bowed submissively. "Your driver assured me that you were unoccupied."

Their furry driver stood just behind the alien greeter. Makl tossed a dirty look Ifruum's way. Wearing an oddly-shaped black cap with a glossy brim, the shaggy alien mocked him with a salute. He'd get him back later. Makl turned his attention back to the nervous being at the car door. "I'll forgive you this one time."

"And you are?" the alien asked.

Angling his chin in the air, he adopted an offended expression. "Like you didn't recognize me. I am the great and wonderful Makline'uum Su'perdio. Supreme ruler of seven planets –"

"The richest, most prosperous," Olivia gushed.

"–in the sixty-ninth galaxy. Don't let your awe strike you blind. You may address me as your highness. I am expected."

"Indeed you are, your, um, highness. If you and the female would follow me?"

"My fiancée has a name," Makl growled, sliding from the aircar, the arm banded around her waist dragging her along with him. Before the male could say anything, he added, "However, I forbid you from using it, or referring to her at all. It is bad enough you got a glimpse of her legs. I am the jealous sort and you wouldn't want me to get the wrong idea. I killed the last male who stared into her eyes."

"I will do my best to avoid all contact, your highness." The creature with the spindly arms and legs scrabbled back, head bowed. "If you will follow me, we have just a few things to do before you may enter the showroom. Trivial security matters that a high-ranking emperor as yourself understands, I'm sure."

Was there truly a more enjoyable role than that of pompous leader? Makl sniffed loudly. "I was informed of your *protocols*." He made the word sound dirty. "And I am going on the record now as saying I am not happy that I was forced to come here without my personal guards or anything more than a gun."

"Which they will ask you to relinquish, your highness, along with any other weapons. It's part of our security procedure."

"It's an outrage," Makl spat. "Treating me like a common thief. If my sweet, delicate sun hadn't begged me for this bauble, I would never put up with it."

"Oh, snookums, don't let the rude man make you change your mind."

"It better be worth it," Makl groused.

"My master makes treasures that are one of a kind."

"Beautiful pretties," gushed Olivia. "And I so want one. Please, my royal delight, I shall be ever so *grateful* if you get me one," she said, dragging a finger down his arm.

"How grateful?" he asked, leaning in.

"Very. Very. Grateful." Her voice dropped to a husky whisper and he closed the distance, kissing her. He could have lied and said he did it as part of their act, but a male could only resist so much. By the universe, she tasted so sweet. Too sweet. Sweet as in stand there all day, sucking on her tongue while his cock seesawed her cleft and wrung a record number of orgasms from her.

Frukx. Enough. He couldn't get distracted, no matter how pleasurable. He had a mission to finish, and a pretty bauble to fetch.

Breaking off the embrace, he stroked her full lower lip with his thumb. He almost went in for another taste. She looked so delectable. A female any male would want to own. In other words, perfect for the role. *Perfect for me.*

"Will you get it for me?" She clasped her hands at her breasts, and peered at him with soft eyes.

Damn, how did she make something so simple look so sensual? *I will give you anything.*

He coughed. "How can I be assured of my, I mean, my fiancée's, safety?"

"There is nowhere safer on this planet, nay, the universe, as my master's shop. Come and you will see. We are completely impregnable. No one comes without invitation, not thief, or assassin, or even client. Everyone goes through a rigorous screening, even the staff."

Makl already knew that. The jeweler made the mistake of boasting to all who listened that he was burglar proof. Murphy couldn't resist the challenge, and Makl volunteered immediately because a feat such as this would make his fame all the greater.

"If anything happens…" Makl let a cold smile with pointed teeth finish the sentence. Three mouths clapped shut. He tossed his pistol and a few knives on the counter for show. He begrudgingly gave up the hidden stiletto in his boot when the guard frisking him found it, and then passed a detector for complex metals. Olivia, giggling and chiding them for scanning her private lady places, had no problems whatsoever. Just as they'd planned.

Done with the first checkpoint, she once again linked her arm in his as they strode after the three-legged alien, Makl's cloak swirling around his boots.

The second checkpoint dealt with spitting and donating a drop of blood to check for nanobots and toxins. They passed easily. Leaving that station, Makl twined his arm around Olivia's waist as they followed the skittering alien further into the building. She slid her arm past the fabric of his cloak to drape along his lower back. She leaned into him and tilted her face up. "How much longer until we get to see the pretties? I'm getting bored."

Oh, she was good. "Not long, my precious. We shall find you the biggest ring they have."

"Forget big, I want the most expensive one. Unless you don't think I'm worth it." Her lower lip jutted in a pout and he almost stumbled he found it so attractive. He kissed the tip of her upturned nose and laughed softly when her eyes crossed.

"Worth every credit this universe has to offer. And if it's not enough, then I shall go to war again and conquer you a new galaxy."

"Just for me?" She batted her lashes.

"Just for you. You know I would give you the universe. All the stars and moons. Every jewel in existence. I would give it all just to make you happy."

She tittered. "Oh, purple pookums, I just want you, and that ring. Oh, and maybe some earrings. I know how you like it when I bedazzle my vault down below." She winked, and this time, their escort stumbled.

The more they bantered, falling into their role of besotted rich alien and his doting female, the more fun Makl had. He'd never had the opportunity to work with a partner, never imagined the enjoyment he could have playing a part, especially the role of lover. The thing that should have frightened him was the fact it didn't require much acting on his part. Everything he did and said came naturally, and from the heart. Sure, it was couched in more flowery terms than he'd actually use, but apart from the grandiose claims and ridiculous nicknames, the way they touched and kissed as they got into character, it was all too easy to believe.

Yet, as much as he found himself focusing on her, he also paid attention to what went on around them. He had to. They played a deadly game of chance. One misstep could prove their last. One wrong move and Olivia could get hurt, or killed. Makl wouldn't allow that to happen. Why the thought of her coming to harm filled him with a cold rage, he couldn't have said, but he embraced it nevertheless.

They passed security points with ease – the malfunction in one caused when part of her skirt got sucked into the scanner, jamming it and exposing her legs – which led to him having a fit, which resulted in them getting ushered quickly, perhaps too quickly, through the next two checkpoints – sealed the jeweler's fate. They were in.

And now came the second act.

*

Olivia didn't recall ever enjoying a heist more. Sure, she and Ifruum had pulled off dozens of gigs in the past. Big thefts, small ones. Some that required acting, others simply nimble fingers. But the thing she recalled most from them all was the nervousness, the fear of getting caught and concentrating constantly on not forgetting her role.

None of that proved an issue with Makl. For some reason, having the big mercenary at her side, even silly as he sounded, acting the role of besotted – and believable – lover, brought her a confidence she didn't quite understand.

Why did he make her feel so safe? So protected? Why did she know that at the first hint of danger, he'd act and save them both? Surely she didn't trust him that much already? Trust or not, though, he made everything flow like an unobstructed breeze. He navigated the twists thrown their way with natural instinct. The purple killer with the deadly body was a natural born actor. Hell, he even had her believing he was madly in love with her. A good thing she knew they played a game, else she might have fallen for his faked smoldering glances, his loving touches, and his ardent embraces.

In retrospect, she was glad he'd eased her earlier sexual tension, or else, in the state he was creating with his innocent caresses, she might have come at an inopportune moment, like when he dropped to his knees in the shop, grasped her right hand, and stared her in the eyes.

They'd made it to the final stage. The inner sanctum of the jeweler, an ugly corpulent being who waddled forth, panting to hand a large box to Makl for inspection. Out he pulled a sparkling monstrosity, and she meant ugly. A band of gold disappeared under the shadow of the precious stone, which winked at her. Holy crap. The thing must have weighed a few good pounds.

Makl clasped her hand and held the beastly jewel above it. "My darling. Goddess of my heart. The one I cherish above all others. I realize this ring can never surpass your beauty or the wealth of what I feel for you, but would you accept it and have it be the token you show the universe as a symbol of our never ending love?"

"Oh, snookums, of course I will." On slid the ring, Makl's fingers deftly sliding it past her knuckle, the weight of the stone dragging her hand down. The rock was bloody huge and dwarfed her fingers. "I shall cherish this ring and you forever."

Makl beamed. "Excellent. You've made me the happiest male alive. I can't wait for my other wives to meet you. I am sure they're going to love you."

And now came the fun part. Olivia pulled back, yanking her hand from his grasp, features twisting into an indignant expression. "Other wives?

Excuse me? Would you mind explaining what you mean by that?"

"I'd say it was pretty obvious. I said I can't wait for you to meet my other wives. The other shining stars in my universe."

"You have a harem?"

"Of course. A male like myself can't restrict himself to just one female, not when I have so much love to give. But don't worry, I have plenty of room in my schedule for you. And when I'm not around, caring for my growing brood will keep you busy and thinking of me."

Up she shot, standing toe to toe with him, her ring finger poking his chest. "I don't think so. Either you divorce those women or I'm leaving."

"Divorce my eleven wives and leave my thirty-six children fatherless?" His eyes went wide.

She bit her tongue as she tossed her head. "If you love me, you'll do it."

He grasped her by the upper arms. "Ask me anything but that."

She pummeled at his chest, her tiny fists getting caught in his cloak, the ring snagging in the fabric. "You jerk. I thought you loved me. That I was the only one."

The shopkeeper looked on in consternation, wringing his hands. "Perhaps you need time to think about this?"

"Stay out of this," they both shouted.

Olivia yanked the ring off and shoved it at the jeweler. "Looks like you're keeping it. I find myself no longer needing it. The engagement is off." Away she flounced, head held high.

"But darling, what happened to loving me forever?" Makl called as he chased after.

She didn't stop her angry stomp.

Through all the checkpoints they flew, arguing and fist-shaking. She even cried at one point, collapsing against a guard who couldn't shove her through his checkpoint quick enough. In less time than it took to enter, they were ensconced in the aircar and headed back to the ship. They did so in silence, listening for pursuit, adrenaline making her heart race.

Only once the bay doors closed did Makl break the silence. "Did you do it?"

"Of course I did." With a grin from ear to ear, Olivia leaned forward and deftly pulled the ring free from the pocket in his cloak. "I've never had an easier switch."

"I wondered if all that groping paid off. It certainly worked for me." He leered and waggled his brows.

She giggled, a mirth that grew and grew until she practically shook with it. Makl didn't appear offended; rather, he smiled broadly as if he enjoyed the sound of her enjoyment. An odder male she'd never met. Most men would have huffed and puffed, demanding to know why she laughed. His ego, though, knew no bounds. Insult him and he somehow saw it as a compliment. Call him a psychopath or a killer and he begged for her to repeat it to everyone she met. Rebuff his sexual advances and he took it in stride, treating it like foreplay. It just never occurred to him she wouldn't want him. Worse, he was right. She'd never known a male so unafraid to speak his mind, no matter how warped his views. Never encountered anyone so full of confidence and life. She'd never met anyone like him, and this drew her more than it logically should.

Yet, there were other times she had to wonder if he was completely off his rocker – and battle an urge to kill him. For example, not even ten minutes later as they relaxed in his room while Ifruum took them out of there. Makl flipped through the news channels of the planet they'd just robbed, waiting for the announcement of the theft. They exited the galaxy without a single news bulletin. Olivia silently cheered. They'd pulled the scam off without a hitch, and without fanfare. This, for some reason, pissed Makl off to no end.

"How can I get famous if no one knows I did the crime?" he groused as he paced the length of the room they shared. Sitting cross-legged on his bed, Olivia paused in her admiration of the ring, and the money it would bring, and threw him a look of incredulity.

"Are you serious? Why would you want people to know it was you? Isn't the whole point to planning the perfect crime getting away clean?"

"Yes, but how am I supposed to attain notoriety if no one knows it was I who bested them?"

"You want them to know you did it?"

"Of course. How else will I achieve fame?"

She gaped at him, blinking in astonishment for a few minutes. When she didn't reply, he turned back and angrily flipped through channels again, muttering nonsense. Her big purple killer wanted to leave a trail. It made her think of the comics she used to read back on earth. Of course, Makl was less

Captain America and more the guy trying to take over the world in black spandex, but hotter. "If you want people to notice you, then you need to start leaving a calling card. Something they can find once the dust has cleared and you've made a clean getaway."

"A business card?" He rubbed his chin thoughtfully. "I guess that might work. It would need to be fireproof and waterproof, though, as I don't always leave the scenes intact."

She wanted to slap herself when he took her literally. "Not a real card, idiot, something unique to you. Like Zorro with his slashed zeee. Or Batman with his mask and toys."

"I know not of whom you speak."

Of course he didn't. Those were references to Earth culture. She did her best to explain.

By the end of it, he sported a wrinkled brow, but his eyes held a thoughtful cast. "So I must find something iconic by which I will be recognized."

"Exactly."

"A unique factor to my escapades that will make me stand out and showcase my greatness."

She rolled her eyes, but nodded her head.

"Now why isn't that in the handbook?" he queried aloud, but to no one in particular, she'd wager.

The door to his room slid open without warning and Makl pivoted, relaxed pose instantly submerged by a warrior ready for action. He had his gun out and pointed at Ifruum before her friend had taken two steps in.

"You should knock," Makl growled, the jokester of moments before replaced by a steel-eyed killer. Funny how she could forget this side of him most of the time, but when the tough mercenary appeared...talk about sexy.

Ifruum ignored the pointed weapon and strolled in further. "Knocking is for the polite, mercenary rule number –"

"You don't need to quote the rules to me. I am well aware of them. I take it you have a reason for barging in. Brave of you considering I might have been debauching your not-so-virgin partner."

Ifruum frowned. "It occurs to me that as her kind-of guardian, I should perhaps question your intentions toward her."

"Dishonorable." Makl replied with a grin.

Leaning forward, Olivia swatted him, her cheeks hot.

Ifruum nodded. "Good to know. I'll assume you're not planning to kill her?" Ifruum asked.

"No. I still need to drop her off at my cousin's to play nanny."

"Maybe," she chimed in.

"Oh, most definitely. I am not going to tell my Aunt Muna that I had a human in my grasp and lost her."

"She'll keep her word," Ifruum said with a wave of his paw. "Right after we make a few more pit stops, eh? I've planned us a fun itinerary on the way to your cousin's, if you don't mind."

"I do mind if they're going to be as useless as the last one." Makl pouted, which should have looked stupid on a grown man, but made her want to kiss the jutting lower lip.

"How can you say our mission was useless?" She held up the ring and let it glint in the light. "It was a complete success. I mean, look at what we got. It's priceless."

Not impressed, Makl shrugged. "Another piece of jewelry. Who cares? I've got crates of them. I steal rare items for the glory and challenge. With no glory, there is no point."

"So, you want to get noticed?" Ifruum stroked his fuzzy chin, and Olivia didn't trust the cunning look in his eye. Not one bit.

"Of course I want to be noticed. I am the Galactic Conqueror."

"I thought it was Avenger," she remarked with a roll of her eyes.

"I changed my mind."

"I thought that was only a woman's prerogative."

"Where did you learn something crazy like that?" he asked. "It is females who are most stubborn and least likely to budge, and us males who are most inclined to change our minds. You humans are so backwards." He shook his head.

Once again, she didn't understand what erratic path his thought process went through, but damn if it didn't entertain her.

"If you get a nickname, then so do I," Ifruum interjected.

"How about Blood Sucking Fanged Wulfen?" Makl tossed grandly.

Ifruum rubbed his chin. "Not bad, but I was thinking more along the lines of something short and simple. Like Fluffy, or Spot."

"Ferocious Spot it is." Makl beamed and Ifruum's tongue lolled. Once again, Olivia wanted to smack herself in the forehead. Then again...if she couldn't beat him, join him. "What should my name be?"

"How about Galactic Concubine?"

"Um, no, I think I'll pass. How about the Lissome Vixen?"

"How about selecting something in a language we can all understand?" Makl scoffed, his vocabulary apparently limited – probably from alien steroid use. "No, I think we should go with the Galactic Pink Portal to Bliss." Makl winked.

She just about choked. "Um, how about the Galactic Bitch who is going to kick your ass in a minute?"

Makl smiled and beckoned with a finger for her to try.

Ifruum sighed. "Are we back to the fighting? Really? And here I thought you'd finally come to an understanding."

Olivia planted her hands on her hips and glared at Makl, whose ice blue eyes dared her. "We did. I understand he's an idiot."

"And she's horny again. It's easy to spot once you know the signs," Makl stated in a serious voice, not breaking the stare. "She starts haranguing and getting contrary. It's really quite adorable. I then tell her how to fix her problem. Lucky for her, my agility in the bedroom is such a cure-all. I point that out. She insists she hates me. I prove her wrong and we start all over."

Heat rushed to her cheeks as she sputtered. "I do not do anything of the sort. You –you –jerk! I hate you!"

"Sure you do." Placating purple asshat, always so full of himself.

She slugged him in the gut, or meant to, but he caught her hand and yanked her close. "See what I mean? You know you can't actually hope to hit me. You just did that so I'd grab a hold of you. But you know, barbarian, you could have asked me to hold your hand. I'm more than happy to get *close*." He winked.

"I am not trying to get close to you," she lied through gritted teeth. Yeah, the words came from her mouth, but she didn't move away. Her body didn't even make a pretense of fighting his allure and stayed where it was, pressed against him.

"Is that a challenge? You know I love a challenge."

She didn't know what she would have said or done next because Ifruum interrupted them.

"Hey, you two, shut up for a second and check this out. You made the news! You both did."

"We did?" The announcement startled Olivia from her semi-wrestling match with Makl.

Makl turned downright gleeful. "This is excellent. Which channels are running it?"

"Most of the ones for this section of the galaxy. See for yourself."

Flipping through several news channels, Makl beamed as the headlines popped up.

The Necking Duo strike again.

Purple and Ivory, the new colors of love – or are they truly broken up? You decide.

The Galactic Lovebirds in what now seems to be a pattern have robbed the famed jeweler…

As he channel surfed from tidbit to tidbit, Makl chortled aloud at some of the wild claims, and exclaimed about the horrible lens angle from the security cameras. The reports and headlines grew wilder.

Olivia sat down and groaned. "Oh my God, we're Thelma and Louise."

"Who?"

"She means Bonnie and Clyde," Ifruum added.

She frowned. "Who?"

Grinning in a manner that surely didn't bode well, Makl declared, "Who cares? We're famous."

"Ugh, but they're calling us the Galactic Lovebirds."

A moue of annoyance twisted Makl's lips. "Yes, I would have preferred they stick to my more public name, but I'm sure my media relations agent can clear that up."

"You have a media relations guy?"

"Of course. And a business manager. All good mercenaries do. How else are we going to get our contracts? I get famous through deeds, which my marketing expert then announces to the world, thus driving up the price of my services. Once you hit a certain level of notoriety and fluid currency, it's just good business sense to have someone managing your affairs and money."

Good grief. Makl was a businessman, an assassin businessman with a marketing pimp and accountant. It boggled the mind. "Aren't you worried the guy in charge of your money will screw you over?"

The smile Makl gave her – dark, menacing, and gleeful – shouldn't have sent a shiver down her spine, she abhorred violence, after all – but delight her it did as well as shoot a tingle to her pussy. He looked so dark, dangerous, and tempting, what woman could have resisted? She did. Barely, but only because she left the room.

As Ifruum and Makl cackled over the unexpected fame they'd found – and discussed ways of cashing in on it – she hit the bathroom, eager to get the heavy hairpiece off and shower. While she stood under the hot water, she pondered the strange turn her life had taken in just the last few days. She'd met a man who attracted her and gave her ridiculous pleasure, and embarked on an adventure that had her heart pounding, but also saw her laughing more than she could recall. Despite the oddity in their thinking, with Makl she found someone to talk to that wasn't like a big brother, or an uncle. It hadn't escaped her notice over the years that in some ways furry Ifruum reminded her of her uncle Murphy, not that she would tell him that. Comparing Murphy to a hairy Chewy when he considered himself so slick and suave probably wouldn't go over well.

She wondered what Murphy thought of Makl. Then wondered why she cared. If only she could talk to someone about the weird shit going on in her head. Despite the crazy factor, she even wished her flaky aunt Karma would pop in for a visit, but she'd gone off on one of her adventures and wasn't answering any of her calls. Who did that leave for Olivia to talk to about how Makl confused the hell out of her? Who could explain why a male who should have been easy to reject and resist instead continually melted all her defenses?

Surely the effect on her wouldn't last forever? It couldn't. He intended to drop her off at some point on that cousin of his. One way or another, this wild ride would eventually end. Now if only she could figure out why the thought depressed her. *Because I can't care for him.* She barely knew him, and had no intention of getting to know him better. Well, better than she already did, but that was just sex. Sex was easy. It was the emotional stuff a girl needed to steer clear of. Olivia knew how caring led to pain. How trust led to betrayal. She wasn't going to make that mistake again.

When she emerged from the bathroom, still no clearer on how she felt about the mercenary, she automatically searched him out. The empty room gaped and her shoulders sagged. For some reason, she'd expected to see him, lounging on the bed wearing a come-hither smile, a taunt waiting on his lips, because he'd pegged it right earlier. She did purposely goad him. She did dare him in the hopes he'd take the decision out of her hands and give her what she wanted, but couldn't ask for. It peeved her off that he'd seen through her subtle game, a game she didn't even realize she played until he pointed it out. How dare he know her better than she knew herself? It was hard to hold onto her image of him as buffoon when he kept showing a rare perception.

Dropping the towel, she padded naked to the wall, looking for a clean shirt. She didn't make it. Arms wrapped around her from behind and she squeaked, limbs immediately flailing.

Makl whispered in her ear. "Hello, barbarian. You smell nice."

"And you just scared the hell out of me. Where were you hiding?"

"Under my cloak."

"Why?"

"To surprise you."

He'd succeeded. She also took note of a more crucial fact. "Are you naked?"

"Very. Wanna see?"

Actually, she did. She turned in his arms as he pushed back the hood of his cape, breaking the invisibility glamour and showing himself, all of his muscular, naked self. His hands returned to clasp the tops of her hips. She didn't move away. She slid her hands under the silky fabric of his cloak to fan them across his chest, thumbing the hoop piercing his pectoral muscle. "And why did you want to surprise me?"

"Well, see, at first, I wanted to see if you'd touch yourself if you thought you were alone."

"And you planned to watch?"

He nodded.

God, why did the thought excite her so much? "What changed your mind?"

"I didn't want to be just a spectator."

"Feeling cloudy-minded again?" She referenced his mercenary law, or rule, or whatever the fuck it was he liked to quote. It served to remind her that what they shared was just sex. Nothing more. Just a physical need.

"I could use some clarity, yes."

"Why not ask one of your – how many wives did you say you had?"

His lips quirked. "Too many for any male to stay sane."

"So you're not married or dating a whole squadron of women in real life?" She didn't look him in the eye when she asked mostly because she didn't want him to know how much his answer interested her.

He shuddered, the tremor clear to the hands she still had splayed on his chest. "By the universe, no. I don't believe in relationships."

"At all?"

"They're a distraction a mercenary can't afford. And a weakness our enemies can exploit."

"Let me guess, it's one of the rules." She really needed to get her hands on a copy of this so-called mercenary manual.

"Not really. The book doesn't cover females and relationships, but I've been around enough to heed the warning. Some choose to ignore it and mate. I, however, don't have that inclination whatsoever."

"So, woman are just for sex?"

"Essentially."

"You won't try and tie me down because we keep getting naked? Or go into some jealous fit because some guy talks to me?"

For a moment, the expression in his eyes turned cold and icy. "Of course not. A female is a female, even exotic ones like yourself."

"Good to know. I wouldn't want you to cry when we have to part."

Again, a glint of something flashed in his gaze, there one second, gone the next. "I shan't even wave goodbye when I drop you off."

"Perfect. Then I guess there's no reason not to have sex, you know, to keep our minds clear and all."

"We have to follow the rules for success."

For a moment, they stared at each other, words she wasn't ready to say sitting heavy on her tongue. His eyes flashed emotions at her, too quick for her to discern. Nothing was said, but the moment exploded.

They dove on each other, lips and teeth clashing in a wild melee involving tongues, panting, and the frantic groping of naked skin. They ended up in bed, Olivia on top of Makl, her wet pussy pressing against his throbbing cock.

"You are in desperate need of clarity, I see," he panted in between the licking of her nipples.

She clawed his shoulders. "Very. And I can see just how stupid you've become. Let me fix that for you." She lifted herself to a seated position, then a little higher until she hovered over the tip of him. His hands splayed across waist and hips, the dark contrast of his mauve skin against hers striking. Sexy. And hot. So hot. With a slow sensuality, he stroked her skin as she lowered herself onto his length. She dug her fingertips into the flesh of his chest as she took him, inch by thick inch, seating herself on his dick and loving it. Only once she had him completely sheathed did she open her eyes only to have his expression steal her breath.

His smoldering, half-shuttered eyes caught her. He gazed upon her like a man starving. Eyed her as if he intended to brand her soul. It was so easy for her to imagine he watched her like a man in love. A man who…

With a cry, she broke the stare and threw her head back, rocking on his shaft, driving him deep inside with circular, grinding movements. He hissed, his fingers tightening on her waist, but not hurting.

Never hurting. He always tempered his deadly strength – treated her like she was fragile and precious.

She almost sobbed her pleasure as she gyrated faster and faster. Her chest heaved with exertion, her breasts bouncing in time to her movement. Impossible as it seemed, he grew even thicker, stretching the walls of her channel, increasing the coiling ecstasy building inside.

"Oh God, purple."

"Give it to me, my beautiful barbarian. Don't hold back. Don't hold –"

With a bellow, he thrust furiously up, and as she rode his bucking body, she cried out, her own pleasure overwhelming. Wave after wave of bliss crashed through her, then crested again as he creamed her with his own orgasm, the hot, pulsing heat stimulating her pussy. Overcome, she sank on top of him, limp and breathing hard. Heart to heart, their frantic beatings somehow crashed in rhythm. Never had she felt closer to someone. More in tune. Damn.

Just sex my ass.

Chapter Ten

~~~~~~

Several successful heists later...

The bad feeling started about halfway through the fleecing they were conducting on a dirty rat – just over five shuddering feet tall and unbathed for several years, judging by his matted fur – which she could have sworn rippled as if something tunneled under its scraggly surface. Olivia's nose twitched, her stomach roiled, and not just because of the rancid smell.

Something is off. Over the years, she'd come to trust her gut instinct. It always saved her tail, something the rodent-like criminal in front of her was missing. Someone shaved his pride and joy a while back judging by the scarred tissue marring the stubby tip of his tail.

Welcome to their newest gig. Currently disguised as a one-eyed, multi-patched, hobble-legged, leering, toothless pirate – and she as his overtired, losing her hair, rotten tooth wench – Makl haggled with the rodent they'd come to see. She felt no remorse in stealing from the smuggler, not when she knew the despicable things he'd done. The small fee they were earning for this mission, which involved planting evidence, wouldn't come close to paying for their trip, but the challenge and satisfaction they'd get in punishing the disgusting alien for what he'd done more than made up for it. If she was going to screw someone over, then let it be the scum of the galaxy.

There was only one big flaw with that, though. The scum were the most paranoid and violent. Makl sensed the same turning tide, she'd wager, because he suddenly tried to wrap things up with less finesse than usual.

"It's time we were on our way. Debauching to do and all that. Perhaps we'll continue this conversation the next time I'm in this section of the star system." She didn't need Makl's subtle finger wag to start making her way to the door through which they'd entered. The rough habitat where they met the rodent was just one of thousands on the surface of this planet. It didn't have much room to maneuver, or extra exits, which was a really poor design flaw, she decided, as she backpedaled quickly. It seemed most prudent given the two large lizard men armed with big guns who pushed their way in and blocked the only way out.

Yet, it wasn't the pair with their rounded sabers, yellow slitted stares, and long green muzzles – very like a crocodile from earth – that made her curse a streak, but the six others who popped up behind and to the side of her from hidden entrances into the room, a pair of doorways hacked into the very walls and covered with holograms they'd missed. She couldn't believe she'd not guessed at their presence. *We're surrounded.* Fuck.

"They ambushed us."

"Not really," Makl replied. "I knew he'd try this."

"You knew and yet you came anyway? Are you insane?" she hissed, just as the lights flickered, a warning sign of the blackout soon to follow.

"Must I answer this question each time we go on a mission?"

"I keep asking because you don't reply, just lead us into more danger without warning."

"Why would I worry you? Have we not escaped unscathed thus far?"

"Yes. But how long do you think that will last?"

"It ends today!" their rodent host yelled, appearing somewhat put out that they ignored him whilst they enjoyed a little spat. Truthfully, they did face danger on pretty much every mission. None of it ever slowed Makl down. The man never broke a sweat, during heists at least. In bed, though…

As if reading her last thought, Makl lifted her hand and kissed it. "Give me a moment to take care of this and then we can pursue more *pleasant* matters."

Stumpy interrupted again. "Leaving so soon, oh Galactic Lovebirds? And yet, the act is not yet done. You haven't yet acquired your prize."

"I see word of our exploits has traveled more quickly than I thought. That's excellent news." Makl beamed at the knowledge of their fame.

Olivia held back a groan. Shit. If this rat knew who they were, then the danger level just shot through the stratosphere. She might have panicked a little if not for the fact Makl didn't appear discomfited in the least. On the contrary, more at ease than ever, he sat down – points for bravery given the sanitation levels in the place – and twitched his fingers at her. Not ashamed to admit the situation had her freaking – the odds against them much higher than usual – Olivia scurried to his side and didn't protest when he pulled her onto his lap. Her purple mercenary would have a plan to get them out. He always did, usually leaving an unfortunate trail of alien bodies behind. Add to his deadly skill the fact Ifruum monitored the situation – so what if the odds were majorly stacked against them? She knew nothing was ever as it seemed. In some cases, it got worse.

"I guess I should be flattered you chose to visit me next. Imagine my glee when I realized who you were. There is a bounty on your heads," the rodent cackled with a show of rotted teeth. "They're paying a bloody fortune for your capture, dead or alive."

"Really? How much? You know my cousin Tren once had one on his head that was considered priceless. It was said they were offering the ownership and title of emperor for a planet in the seventeenth discovered star quadrant," he confided to Olivia, taking his eyes off their host to speak to her.

She looked for a hidden meaning in his words, but it was real subtle if there because she couldn't figure it out.

"It doesn't matter how much the prize is. It's mine. As is the female. I've seen the videos." Stumpy licked his lips. "I bet I'd make a fortune making a video of my own. Especially if she's a screamer."

"You will not touch my female," Makl said in a light tone, a knife suddenly twirling in his palm.

Olivia wanted to say something in her defense, but honestly, it seemed in her best interest to let the expert in violence do the talking. That and she liked the dark, possessive way he said it.

The stupid rat didn't heed the warning, or the fact a second knife joined the first in spinning in Makl's palm. Small or not, she'd seen them in action. Uncanny how Makl never missed when he tossed the sharp daggers.

"Oh, I will touch her. And bite. And do all kinds of things to her, in color, all recorded. I'll even let you watch if you like while I do it. Then, I'll show the universe."

What, no evil laugh? Olivia knew Makl would lament the lack when he watched the replay of this moment later. He did so like the drama.

A heavy sigh left Makl. "See, my luscious barbarian. They make me do it. I tell him one simple thing. Just one. Don't touch my female, and he argues. Actually, he doesn't just argue, he threatens. Do you know how many mercenary mantras he's crossed? You can't tell me he doesn't beg to die."

Makl still liked to make fun of the fact she flinched over death. Despite their missions, she still didn't quite have his cool attitude toward it. Yet. But neither did she argue with his methods when she thought it justified. Like now. She found her voice. "Oh, he's asking for it alright. I guess this one time, it's okay."

"It is?" Makl's expression brightened and even under the layers of disguise, she could see his glee. It was ridiculously charming.

"Excuse me, Galactic Lovebirds, time to break you up. Guards, grab the mercenary while I take care of the girl."

"Do you want the one on the left?" Makl asked as he stood, setting her to his side while concealing the fact he slid her a gun.

"Which one is that?" she asked, peering around, gnawing her lower lip.

Makl cracked his knuckles and rolled his neck. "On second thought, I'll handle him too. I'm out of practice when it comes to a single focus melee."

Out of practice? The reality of what he implied made her feel faint. "Makl, you can't hope to take them all on. There's like eight of them, nine if you count our two-timing friend, the rat."

"I know, unfair odds. Do you think I should tie an arm behind my back? I don't want it said I'm not making an effort."

The faintness returned, but adrenaline quickly overcame it as some rude henchman interrupted their tête a tête. Makl spun and met the charge; the little knives he drew earlier flashed through the air and hit a lizard – *thunk, thunk.* Down he went and Olivia winced. Damn, he was fast. So fast, Makl already had a new pair of knives suddenly gripped in his hands. The dark blades, without a shine to give them away, spun and slashed. And just like that, two more guards went down.

"Hey, did you know we're on camera? Behind you and to your left. Our host taped the whole meeting. I hope it captured my good side," Makl mused.

Only her purple lover would take the time to contemplate something so trivial. She really had to wonder at how his mind processed things seeing as how he worried more about looking his best as the rest of the guards now charged while ratman screamed, "Kill them!"

He just never changed. Olivia shook her head. "Behind you, purple."

Makl didn't even turn around. He reached back, yanked forward. Slit. Twist. And another body hit the ground. "I wish I'd worn something different. This is not my best look."

Later, she was going to kill him for his nonchalant attitude in the face of death. If they survived. Wait. If they survived...she'd fuck him until he turned from purple to pink. Yeah, because he'd deserve it if he got them out of here alive – and with all her body parts intact.

Just when she thought she might have a heart attack if he didn't pay attention, Makl finally turned to face the bulk of the attack, and Olivia belatedly remembered to peek behind her. It seemed Stumpy's henchmen didn't see her as much of a threat because the pair at her rear seemed more intent on circling around to catch Makl off guard.

Ah, fuck. Despite her aversion to deadly violence, even she knew this wasn't the time for hesitation. Makl was good, but as his partner, she should help. Pretending she was part of a realistic video game, she took a deep breath and raised the pistol Makl gave her. She shot a lizard man in the leg joint. He collapsed with a scream that wouldn't stop and she stared at the writhing creature, horrified.

With a spin and a leap, Makl took care of the strident noise, and then took the time to chide her. "I'm trying to work here, barbarian. We don't play with our prey during battle. We save that for when we have time for torture."

Play? Torture? Was he fucking serious?

Yes, he was. He winked before he dove to the side to avoid the lunge of the remaining guards. Watching him pop up and down – weave, bob, slice, and dice – all the while smiling and running a commentary, Olivia couldn't help summarizing to herself the enigma known as Makl. One, Makl knew his shit. Damn, the man could fight and make it look effortless. He moved like a dancer, his body flexible and fluid, always in motion. Just like his mouth. He never shut up. She'd never heard such taunting in her life. If it weren't for the gravity of the moment, she might have giggled at some of his wilder claims. But the most fucked up thing was her realization he was having fun. Not just fun, but an absolute blast. Odds stacked against him, covered in blood and faced with possible death, Makl was in his glory. She didn't know whether to run while he kept them distracted, help him, or applaud. He clearly didn't need her help. Not with just one guard and the rat left to overcome.

Instinct made her duck, and in the nick of time too. A saber whistled over her head. While she'd wool gathered, reinforcements had arrived. She dove to the ground as she spun. Bodies crowded the door, shorter forms brandishing laser pistols. Crap.

Olivia took quick aim and fired, aiming for their wrists in the hope of knocking out their weapons. However, these new arrivals wore body armor and it absorbed the shots. Uh-oh.

They lunged and she scrambled, but slid in the blood of a dead lizard on the floor. She barely managed a squeak before one thug grabbed her hair and yanked. "Ow!" The newcomer halted her flight and brought her to her knees.

Makl turned in that moment, the tilt of his body revealing Stumpy's visage, glassy-eyed, and very dead, his plot to ambush gone horribly awry. Kind of like their plan. The new arrivals weren't factored into any equation they'd thought of or encountered before. Fuck. They'd not counted on fame bringing them down. Just how high was the darned bounty?

"Step away from the girl." Makl asked nicely as he wiped his blade on a corpse.

"Give yourself up or we hurt the female," a gravelly voice demanded.

Olivia couldn't help a wince as the fist in her hair twisted. Makl's icy gaze narrowed. Big mistake. Someone had challenged her mercenary. He'd never back down now.

"I have a different plan." Makl dropped his hands to lie loosely at his side, the blades pointing down.

Used to his methods, Olivia knew better than to allow his relaxed stance to fool her. He was ready to fight. For her. How hot. "Let my female go and I will let you leave. Alive. It's a good deal. I'd take it."

Unlike the moment before when he uttered words very similar, there was none of the mirth. A serious mien turned Makl's eyes into ice chips. He'd never looked more attractive.

The alien holding her tightened his grip and shook her. She couldn't help a cry of pain from bursting loose. "Do not toy with us, mercenary." Olivia bit her lip, but tears of pain sprang to her eyes when they yanked her head back, exposing her neck to the tip of a sword.

"You really shouldn't have done that."

Icy calm. Deadly serious. Ominous. So very ominous. Olivia shivered at Makl's tone. Someone was about to die. *I just hope it's not me.*

The lights in the place flickered. The hands holding her relaxed a fraction, but only for a moment. They tensed back up quicker and more painfully than before.

"Who's afraid of the dark?" Makl taunted.

And then the lights went out, but didn't come back on.

Chapter Eleven

Rage, a wild, violent storm of wrath took over when Makl saw Olivia threatened. He could see the fear in her wide eyes and the tremble of her lips and he didn't like it one bit.

He blamed himself for her predicament. Focused on showing off and enjoying himself with the rodent's minions, he failed to pay close enough attention to what happened behind him. Olivia currently paid for his lapse.

But most unacceptable of all, he couldn't handle the lines of pain bracketing her mouth and eyes as the ones holding her hostage hurt his delicate barbarian. *How dare they touch her!*

When the lights flickered, Makl took note of everyone's position in the room, so when the room went completely and utterly dark, just another rolling blackout on a planet famous for them, he was ready. In he darted before anyone could react. He used his speed and hopefully the element of surprise to reach his goal.

Having trained in the dark – numerous times as his cousins thought it funny to drop him in the arachnid-infested mines bordering his father's property – Makl relied on his keen senses to guide him. Blades swinging, he didn't allow himself to hesitate or worry about Olivia. He couldn't, not when the slightest pause might spell her doom.

Inhalation to his left. Out shot his fist and he connected with the sharp end of his dagger. Scuff to his right and he swept his foot, the loud thump giving him a position to plunge his knife. A rustle of fabric and he started to swing only to pause mid-arc as his nose twitched at a familiar scent. His incomplete swing reversed and a gush of warm liquid ran over his hand.

On it went for an eternity. For less than a heartbeat.

When the lights came back on, he stood with his weapons dripping wetly while bodies littered the space around him. For a moment, panic fluttered in his breast as he didn't see the one person he wanted most of all. Probably because he straddled her. Makl peeked down and grinned. Olivia, however, didn't grin back. It might have had to do with the layer of grime and guts coating her, though. "I guess it's a good thing I didn't tie that hand behind my back after all," he jested, hoping to snap her out of it.

It worked. Up she sprang. "You crazy, stupid fucking alien. That was insane."

Usually when she yelled at him, she stalked off or called him a few more choice words. He would follow. They'd yell. Fight. Kiss and couple furiously. This time, she broke the pattern. She threw herself at him and hugged him tight before mashing her lips to his. What a shame the blood coating them both had them quickly separating. She gagged and wiped her mouth.

"Oh fuck, that's gross."

"And not too healthy for you either. What do you say we get out of here and grab a shower?"

"What about leaving a calling card? You didn't exactly leave anyone alive to talk to the press or authorities."

"Who gives a frukx if anyone knows? Come." Makl almost slapped himself as he said it. Of course he cared if he got credit, but looking at Olivia coated in blood, a visual reminder of his lapse of attention, he could only think of one thing…well, maybe a few. They all, however, featured her naked in a hot shower and him examining every inch of her for injury before slamming into her, thanking his goddess that she emerged mostly unscathed.

For a moment, when he'd seen her so close to death, a chill unlike anything he'd ever experienced gripped his heart tight enough to stall it. It rattled him still and he needed something to dispel the odd spasm.

First, though, they needed to escape. Exiting the tenement hovel, Makl cursed as he saw a gang of bullies pile out of an aircar. More? Seriously? Had they been under surveillance since their arrival? He'd have to work on that before their next mission. He'd gotten lazy with fame. No more. He shoved Olivia in the direction of his ship and safety, then, he braced for battle. "Run along and find Ifruum while I take care of these ruffians."

"Come *with* me." She tugged at him, the concern in her tone genuine.

He turned his head and leaned. She saw his intent and closed the gap. He kissed her hard. "Warm up the shower for me. I'll be along in a few minutes and I'll be in need of a good *cleansing*." Right after he killed a few aliens.

*

Makl spun Olivia to face away from him and gave her a small push. She staggered a foot, but whirled around in time to see her purple mercenary dash toward the approaching armed gang with a wild yell.

"Who wants to die first?"

Crazy bastard. He just couldn't pass up a chance to kill something, all part of his attempt to surpass his cousin's kill count. And he would have probably succeeded against this bunch if reinforcements didn't suddenly spill from a pair of doorways on either side of him.

Ambush! Despite their short stature, the grey wave of alien newcomers swarmed Makl and he went down under a sea of bodies. She lunged forward, intent on helping him, but a familiar furry arm wrapped around her middle and halted her flight.

"Ifruum, what are you doing?"

"You heard the big purple guy. Getting us out of here."

"But what about Makl?"

"He can take care of himself."

Yes, he could. It didn't mean he should have to, not when he'd jumped in there to save her ass.

"Let me go. I have to help him."

Ignoring her demand, Ifruum dragged her in the opposite direction, where safety awaited. A part of Olivia understood she couldn't help Makl against those kinds of odds. She could shoot, but she couldn't shoot into that roiling ruckus of bodies without possibly hurting Makl. Knew it was madness to even try, but that didn't stop her. She broke free of her friend and dashed back toward the battle, raising her gun and firing on the outskirts, head and upper body shots, forgetting in her fear for Makl her repugnance of killing. She couldn't see her purple lover, but she could hear him. Laughing and taunting. The idiot was still alive.

He fought, which meant they still had a chance.

Or at least Makl did. Olivia's life expectancy, however, dropped quite a few percentage points when the guns came out of nowhere, pointed at her head.

But it was the application of a syringe to her arm that sank her into a black hole, one she didn't know if she'd escape from.

Chapter Twelve

Whistling, Makl returned to his ship, thirty-six kills higher than he'd started his day. A little bit bruised. A touch burned. And covered in gore. But, he'd won. Now, he just needed to leave before the city tried to bill him for damage when they noticed the section of neighborhood he'd accidentally blown up.

Boarding his ship, he practically ran to the command center, eager to see Olivia. Upon entering, he noted Ifruum at his usual post, sans his human. "Where is the barbarian?" Waiting for him naked in his room, he hoped.

"What do you mean where? Isn't she with you?" Ifruum spun in his seat and morphed in to Murphy, his agitation clear to see.

An icy chill halted Makl's tapping fingers mid-launch sequence. "No. Last I saw, she'd met up with you and you were heading back to the ship."

"We were until she decided to go back and help you."

"You let her do what?" Makl's low tone didn't convey any of his rage, but he sure hoped it hid the discordant quaver that swept his body

"I didn't let her do anything. In case you hadn't noticed, that girl does whatever she damned well pleases, and apparently, it pleased her to think she was helping your worthless purple carcass."

"Except I don't recall seeing her at the fight. You either, for that matter."

"Not all of us enjoy blood and mayhem. I knew you'd prevail so I figured I'd stick to the plan and have the ship ready to go."

And go they should. Makl understood that on some level. He'd escaped the danger zone – or at least the imminent part. Once he left the surface of the planet, just another ship heading off into space, he'd be back to planning the next mission. He didn't owe the human anything.

Going back was stupid. Suicidal. He should take off while he had a chance. And yet, several galactic units later, under the cover of darkness, there he was, infiltrating the home of the rogue who stole his human. He could blame it on his ego, his need to best the thief who kidnapped Olivia. But deep down inside, Makl knew the true reason. The real reason.

He did it to save Olivia. Never mind he'd never met a female who vexed him so much. Who engaged his senses on levels he'd never imagined. Who made him question every rule he'd learned. He couldn't ignore the fact she'd come back for him. Faced her repugnance of meting death to help him. Makl couldn't leave her behind, especially when he found out Murphy wouldn't use his special ability to pop in and out of places to save her.

"What do you mean you won't get her?" Makl growled when his information network spit out her location – after the application of a few pointy knives.

In his human shape for their conversation, Murphy shrugged. "I'm a god, not a magician. I can't just change the course of fate when I don't like it. Or teleport more than one person at a time," he grudgingly admitted.

"Then what's your plan to save her?"

"I don't have one. But Olivia knew this was a possibility. Capture always is. It's part of the thrill. You should know that. Although, in losing her, I guess that leaves you minus a human for your cousin. A shame."

"A shame? Who frukxing cares about Tren? We can't just leave Olivia to that debauched alien."

With his connections, it didn't take Makl long to discover who'd taken his human. A local mob lord, not a big time crook, but high enough up the monetary ladder that Makl knew he couldn't just barge in demanding he give Olivia back.

"Why ever not? He's no worse than you, surely."

"Exactly my point." Did someone else try and touch Olivia? Over his dead and cooling body. With vengeance fueling objective, with less planning than he preferred, Makl found himself scaling the wall of a tall structure, an apartment building made of black glass, the best color for blending in. Slimming, too. Suction grips on the soles of Makl's feet and palms of his hands helped him climb, an E.M.P. fuelled force field just outside the structure making any electronic attempt to scale the exterior wall useless. It was grueling, tiring work – for anyone not as strong as he.

Quickly, Makl worked his way up the building to the top floor and the balcony entrance. Heaving himself over the railing, he pressed himself flat on the cold stone and listened. No alarms went off and he didn't hear any indication anyone spotted him. Inching forward, he peered at the small slit of light shining from the curtain drawn over the balcony's glass doors. He couldn't see or hear anything, but the slight thump of bass from music played inside, music that probably hid the sounds of terror as the miscreant did who knew what to his human.

I'm coming to save you, barbarian.

Contemplating his next move – dive through the window in a crashing assault that would look great if caught on film, or sneaking in unnoticed – the choice was decided the moment he heard Olivia's squeal.

One shot to shatter the glass and in he rolled, springing up with his guns pointed, only to stop at the sight meeting his eyes.

Dressed in a silky red robe, clean and holding a glass of sparkling liquid, Olivia didn't appear too terrified. "Makl, what are you doing here?" Olivia gasped.

"Apparently, not saving you from a fate worse than death," was his dry reply. He took one look at the cozy scene – dim lighting, buffet of food, and a bed in the corner – turned on his heel, and strode back out into the cool night air – his temper seething – his chest oddly aching.

*

Olivia scrambled from the couch, astonished and yet stupidly pleased to see Makl. Kajob, an old friend of hers whom she'd worked with a time or two in the past, paused in his recitation of his most recent exploit – one that had her laughing just moments before – eyed her, then the broken patio door.

"I take it you know him?"

"Yes. If you'll excuse me, I need to speak to him." She skirted the broken glass and exited through the billowing curtains to find Makl staring at the night sky.

She hesitated, unsure of what to say. The moment drew out, tense, but she couldn't have said why. She wanted to touch her purple mercenary. Have him face her. Say something. She tucked her hands behind her back and spoke first. "I'm surprised to see you here."

"I don't leave my allies behind."

Huh. Odd, the mercenary manual advised cutting allies who got caught because chances were they'd compromise you. She'd truly expected him to take off the first chance he got – and never look back. "I can't believe you came back for me, purple."

"Well, I wouldn't have if I'd known you didn't need rescuing," was his bitter reply.

If she didn't know better, she'd have said he sounded hurt and a touch jealous. Makl? Her jokester? "But you didn't know that and you came anyway." She put her hand on his arm. The muscle underneath tensed. She didn't let that deter her from stepping closer. "Why did you come? You could have left."

A heavy sigh left him. "I couldn't. Just like you didn't when you had the chance."

She shrugged. "Yeah, well. You know how it is about glory. I couldn't let you hog it."

"So what now?"

"What do you mean?"

"You seemed pretty cozy with your abductor."

She noted how hard he gripped the railing and wondered at the reason. Surely he wasn't jealous? "Afraid of losing your ticket to stardom?"

A muscle jumped in the side of his jaw. He didn't answer for a moment. "You could say that. So, what's it going to be, barbarian? You staying or coming?"

He was giving her a choice? Was this his way of quietly ditching her? If so, then why come back for her in the first place, other than pride?

"Are you still planning to turn me into a nanny?"

"You? A nanny?" Kajob trumpeted his laughter from two of his trunks and snickered with the rest as he joined them on the balcony. "I can't picture it."

"No one was talking to you," Makl snarled.

"Testy fellow, aren't you? We'll see how mouthy you are after my guards are through with you." Out came a big gun aimed at Makl's chest.

"Stop teasing, Kajob." Olivia frowned at the smuggler.

"Who's teasing? Even now, my guards are surrounding him. Escape is impossible."

"You can't capture him. He wouldn't even be here if it weren't for me."

"I know. It's why I snagged you when I got the chance. The perfect bait to snare the other half of the Galactic Lovebirds." Kajob sneered.

"Snare? You mean this was all part of a plan? I thought we were friends."

"For the kind of money being offered for your capture, I'd sell my whole family."

"Why am I not surprised?" Makl muttered, not seeming concerned at all.

She turned her back on Kajob. "I'm sorry, purple. I didn't know he planned this."

"I figured he would, which is why I brought along this."

Before she could scream or ask him to explain, Makl gripped her around the waist and flung them both off the balcony. Down they plunged, air whistling past her ears, her mouth open in a silent scream. Her crazy purple lover, of course, had the time of his life.

"Wheeee!"

Stupid adrenaline junkie. But if he wasn't scared then that meant…

A sudden jolt and their imminent meeting with the ground slowed. He'd brought along a parachute.

For some reason, this struck her as insanely comical and she laughed. Giggled actually, with a note of hysteria.

"I'm glad you find this entertaining," he grumbled as he guided them to a low rooftop.

"It's just whenever I think we're fucked, you pull a rabbit out of your ass and save us."

"I assure you, I did not have anything up my ass." He sounded offended.

She laughed louder. "I didn't mean it literally. I meant… Oh, forget what I meant. Thanks for saving us, again." Feet on solid ground, and no one shooting them for the moment, she plastered a kiss on him, a kiss he devoured with a passion that never failed to excite, no matter how inopportune the moment.

*

"Can you work on tying your tongues in knots later?" an exasperated Ifruum barked from above before they even got to the groping. "We're not out of the woods yet, kids."

No, they certainly weren't. Makl broke away from Olivia and grasping her hand, dragged her to the air car Ifruum *appropriated,* and from none other than their most recent host, Kajob.

Piling into the two-seater with Olivia on his lap, the superfast aerial vehicle made quick work of getting them back to his ship, disguised to look like a mail carrier. Out they slipped, escaping the influence of the mobster. Now, if only Makl could outrun the confusion in his head.

What was wrong with him lately? Making mistakes. Going against the mercenary laws that always guided him.

Olivia was his ally – and lover. But he didn't need her. She brought him some value, but not enough to risk his life, so why did he ignore the smart thing to do and for no compensation, save her?

And why did he keep replaying the chilling moment when in that dirty hovel, the tip of a sword pricked the skin of her fragile neck. One slice, one quick jab, and she could have bled out before his eyes. Died, and he couldn't have stopped it. Sure, he saved her in the end, yet he couldn't escape the chill of that moment.

Even in the shower, the temperature cranked, his cock buried to the hilt, his body curved up against hers, he couldn't shake the cold. The fear.

She almost died. Who cares? I do, it seems. But why? He might have pondered it longer, but she chose that moment to scream his name, "Makl!" and came around his dick, sweet, undulating waves wringing heat and so much more from him.

As for later…well, they discovered many more ways to generate heat and he pushed the feeling away. Forgot it, but at the same time, never repeated his mistake. From there on, he kept her safe from harm – even if he had to delay their missions so he could pop in first and take care of a few potential problems. *I won't let her come that close to harm again.* His heart couldn't handle it.

Chapter Thirteen

The scare he'd suffered faded as they took on lighter jobs, in between having sex. Makl discovered that even without the usual danger, he still had fun. Anything he did with Olivia at his side made him smile.

Lying with his human panting atop him, Makl could say he'd never felt more complete. Or clear-headed. With a rare clarity, he finally grasped the allure of having a constant female in his life. A female who understood and accepted him as he was. A female who didn't fear challenging him at every turn. Who didn't fake her pleasure in bed because he paid her. A partner he could share things with. Someone more than just a lover…someone he wanted to call mate.

Argh!

Up he sprang in a panic, a twinge of remorse almost making him wince when Olivia flew off his body and hit the carpeted floor with a shouted, "What the fuck?"

However, one twinge wasn't enough to stop him from diving off the other side of the sleeping pallet. He grabbed some pants and with a muttered, "I need to check on something," practically ran out of the room, barefoot and shirtless.

Space! He needed alone space to think about what he'd just realized. *I want to keep my human, permanently.* The travesty of it. The horror!

Makl stalked the length of his ship, wondering how he'd let this happen. How did he come to care for a human? How did he let himself stray from his set path far enough that he even thought of keeping her as mate?

Good thing he'd caught on to his problem. Now he could deal with it. *I just won't care for her.* Done.

Or not.

Stray thoughts questioned how he'd accomplish this. How could he stop feeling for the barbarian?

Distance. He needed physical distance. Which meant…*no more sex.*

Hmm, maybe a little too rash. He needed the sex to keep his mind clear. What could he do instead? No more cuddling. Yeah, that was part of the problem, all that arms–around–each–other, snuggling–and–talking stuff had to stop. He never used to do that before. So what if he enjoyed it? He also enjoyed a good rest period and dessert; it didn't mean he couldn't do without. After coitus, he'd have to make sure she kept to her side of the bed.

But was that enough? Judging as how all his pacing circles kept bringing him back to the room they shared, not quite. He needed something a little more drastic. He needed to get away from Olivia and her drugging influence.

Perhaps he should forget going on any more missions? After all, how many times did they pull off a successful heist and barely make it to the ship before tearing at each other and copulating like wild animals? Damn, he'd miss that. Besides, the missions were fun and good for his reputation. Scrap that plan. They'd keep up their crime spree; they'd just have to stop acting like a simpering couple in love.

No more hand holding, or fake – torrid – kisses that led to real ones later on. No more groping as part of the job or for pleasure. He'd have to stop flaunting his body so she'd take advantage – a shame, because she did that so well. From here on in, he'd view her as just another male. An ally, like Ifruum.

With heavy feet, he stomped into the bridge and flopped in his chair.

Murphy's smooth-skinned face peered at him from over the top of a large sheaf of black and white paper. "For a man with no shoes, you're sure making a ruckus."

"What has she done to me?" he groused.

"Done? I assume you speak of my niece, Olivia."

"Yes. Who else?"

"Did she injure you?"

"Not exactly."

"Double crossed?"

"Not yet."

"Told you she was pregnant by another man and asked you to be the baby's daddy?"

"What? Who else has laid hands on her?" Makl practically roared as he leapt from his seat.

Murphy held his hands out in a placating gesture. "Easy, big guy. I was just trying to ascertain the nature of your problem."

Groaning, Makl dropped his face into his hands. "The problem is I like her."

"I should hope so, seeing as how you've been doing things this uncle prefers not to think of."

Makl's head shot up and he scowled. "Yeah, well, it's the things I want to do with her that I've never wanted to do before that worry me."

Up shot Murphy's brows. "I don't know if I'm the right person to talk to about that. If you're wanting something kinky, you'll have to talk to her. Or not. On second thought, let's switch this discussion to the weather. Have you seen that galactic dust cloud in the third quadrant?"

"I wasn't talking about sex stuff. I meant –" Makl paused as he fought to say the words. He waved his hands around and groaned in frustration. "I was talking about emotional stuff."

"Oh, you mean the fact you fell in love."

"I did not." Makl pointed his gun at Murphy's head without even thinking twice. "Take that back."

"You do realize your petty weapon can't harm me? I am a god."

"You might be a god and, yet, you're inching back, which means even if you survive, it will still hurt, sure as hell."

"And they call you the dumb one."

"Who does?"

"No one. Now, what were we talking about? Ah, yes, your –"

The insistent buzz on his console wouldn't be ignored. With a sigh, Makl leaned back in his seat and accepted the call.

"Why are you dawdling?"

Just great. A bad day made worse. He banged his head off the headrest of his seat. "Hello to you too, Aunt Muna."

"Don't *hello* me. We're waiting for you to arrive with the nanny."

"I told you I wasn't anywhere near Earth. These things take time," he deftly lied.

She didn't buy it for a second. "Oh really, and yet, it was just yesterday we watched another video of the newest daring exploit of the Galactic Lovebirds, and what an odd twist of circumstance, but they happen to look like you and a human. A female human."

Frukx. In his quest for fame, he'd forgotten one obvious aspect. "You saw that, did you? How did I look? Did they get my good side? Did Tren see it? Jaro?"

"We've all seen it. And you'll be lucky if Tren doesn't skin you alive when you get here, which I might add, better be quick because he's in a bad mood. I think it's all that pent up anger. This whole keep-quiet-lest-you-wake-the-baby thing has made him a bomb waiting to explode."

"I'm less than a day away." Or would be, once he stopped dallying and taking on the side jobs Ifruum kept sending his way. He needed to face facts. He'd delayed delivering Olivia to his cousin so he could spend more time with her. Another damning clue that should have woken him to the fact she'd gotten too close.

No more meandering. He'd head directly to Tren's and solve his epiphany. Drop off the human and leave. Out of sight, he'd stop craving things he didn't want or need, such as a mate and constant companion. He'd also have to return to his five-fingered daily release too, but maybe that was a good thing given the copulation he'd enjoyed lately didn't leave him clear-headed. On the contrary, he'd never felt more frukxed up. "Prepare the family for my arrival."

"I'll do my best to hold your cousin off, but you might want to make it a short visit. He's a little testier than usual." The communicator clicked off, leaving Makl pondering.

Maybe he wouldn't get off his ship at all once he got to the planet. There wasn't really any point in staying. By departing rapidly, he'd avoid a messy goodbye with the barbarian – who would obviously miss him immensely given his innate greatness, which in turn would make her cry and beg him to stay – and he'd avoid his cousin and his cousin's mighty fist. A perfect plan. Foolproof.

Murphy rustled his paper as he folded it. "So, you still intend to have Olivia play the part of nanny?"

Ah, frukxing hell. Had Murphy heard his last thought? Hopefully not. He needed to get away, to continue on his path to greatness – by himself. "Alas, the Galactic Lovebirds have had their final act. My family needs her so it's time to drop her off."

"Just ditch her like yesterday's news, eh?" Murphy cocked a brow and Makl tamped down the heat threatening his cheeks.

"It's not like we promised anything to each other. We both knew it wasn't permanent. I'm a mercenary. She hates the fact I'm a killer. And Tren needs her. It was fun while it lasted."

"Yes, it was, and I am sure she'll see it that way when you cast her off without even so much as a wave goodbye. And what will you do next? You've lost half of your gimmick. What lies in the Galactic Loner's future?"

Loner?

The word struck a discordant note. Left a sour taste in Makl's mouth, even though he didn't reply. He couldn't have said why. The word loner described him perfectly. It was the life he ascribed to. The life laid out in his mercenary handbook. A life that stretched bleakly without the laughter and adrenaline he'd gotten used to.

"It's not a weakness to admit you need her," Murphy said quietly.

Need her? Makl opened his mouth to say he didn't need her. He didn't need anybody. However, the words stuck to his tongue. The lie wouldn't allow itself to be spoken.

"Stubborn fool. Suffer then. I'm going to check on a few pies I've got my finger in." Murphy disappeared, not that Makl paid him any mind. Not anymore. The pesky god was always somewhere underfoot these days, it seemed, in one guise or another. Besides, he discovered something more pressing to occupy his attention as it occurred to him that he had very little time left with his human. Very little time to enjoy her body and laughter. What could it hurt to let himself sink into her one last time?

Since he'd leave her shortly, he owed it to her to assuage her lust so that she didn't start her new job mentally incapacitated. Sometimes, his generosity surprised even him.

Returning to his room with due haste, he could understand why Olivia rebuffed his kiss in order to give him a totally undeserved harangue.

"What the hell, Makl? You can't just throw me off the bed, run off, and then come back and expect sex."

"I needed to check on something."

"Gee, I hadn't noticed. You know, though, if you needed to get up, you could have just said so," she complained. "No need to dump me on my ass." A line creased her brow. "Is something wrong? Anything I need to know about?"

"Nothing important. But I think we should check out the temperature level of the shower again."

"Really?" Her lips quirked. "Has it stopped working since the last time?"

"Quiet, barbarian, and just do as you're told." Unable to resist, he slapped her bottom, but instead of squeaking and rolling away, Olivia let out a little moan of pleasure and pushed up onto her hands and knees. She tossed him a coy look over her shoulder.

"I guess then you'll have to punish me, because I'm not listening." She waggled her buttocks at him.

Saucy barbarian. By all the stars, he would miss her. His hand flashed out and slapped a rounded cheek. It hit with a loud smack. Her flesh jiggled and she dropped her upper body to the mattress, in effect projecting her rear higher, spreading herself to his view.

At the sight of her pinkness, moist and inviting, Makl couldn't tear his trousers off fast enough. He kneaded the soft flesh of her cheeks and knelt on the bed behind her, pressing his mouth against the shell like core of her sex.

The flavor of her, a nectar more delectable than anything he'd ever tasted, hit his tongue and he closed his eyes in pleasure. Groaned, as well. Over the past little while, he'd gotten to know her body quite intimately. Enjoyed every inch of her – more than once – and yet, he never tired of anything, not her taste, reaction, or the feel of her skin.

Like a drug, he always wanted more. And more. And…

Latching onto her clit, he stroked it with his lips and tongue, hearing her approaching climax in the shortness of her pants, the way her moans emerged, low and desperate. He tore his mouth away and heard her utter a lamenting protest. Up onto the bed he crawled, between her spread thighs. His arm slid around her waist as his cock slammed into her welcoming heat. He pumped her urgently, curving her body back so they were flush to each other, his dick driving while his fingers played. One hand on her cleft stroked her clit, the other thrummed her erect nipples. His lips sucked at the tender skin of her neck, that pale, unblemished expanse of temptation.

She came with a scream, her sex milking his shaft, pulling forth his orgasm. But he didn't yell his bliss. Instead, he clamped his teeth, not too hard, but enough that when they separated their sweating bodies to flop on the bed, she wore a mark on her flesh. His mark.

It looked good on her.

And she was leaving. Soon.

Into the shower he carried her to take her again, needing to brand her in every way possible.

If she sensed a desperation in his caresses, in the way he worshipped and took her body, she didn't say. Makl, however, found himself all too aware of the ticking clock counting down to their separation.

Forget sleep, his mind remained alert, focused on her, memorizing her every expression, every pant, curve, aspect.

Spent and entwined upon his bed, he held her, unable to sleep. He couldn't help reliving the time they'd spent together, their talks and adventures. He knew so much about her, the Olivia of today and now, and yet so little of her past. A past she never spoke of.

It bothered him all of a sudden. Who was this female he brought into the bosom of his family? How had she ended up where she had in space? And adopted by Murphy, a god? It became the most important thing in that moment – as she lay cradled in his arms, her head nestled on his chest. He had to know, had to hear her tale. "How did you end up in space as Murphy's ward?"

A bitter chuckle made her body shake. "Oh, now there's a post coital bedtime story. Why would you want to hear that sad tale?"

"Curiosity." A need to understand her he couldn't explain. And so she told him her story – and he made a list of beings to kill, new enemies he made a priority to eradicate – free of charge.

Chapter Fourteen

〜〜〜〜〜〜〜〜〜〜〜〜〜〜〜〜〜〜〜〜〜〜〜〜〜〜〜〜〜〜〜〜〜

"Look, Mommy. There are lights in the sky." A much younger Olivia craned her neck, fascinated by the sight of a perfect ring of white light bursts hanging amidst the backdrop of a dark galaxy rife with stars. In the city, the stars rarely shone so clearly, and she'd never seen anything like the glowing circle.

"It's probably just an airplane."

Airplanes sported red taillights and moved quickly. This anomaly proved stationary. "But it's not moving. Actually, the lights are getting closer." Definitely not typical aviation behavior, even ten year-old Olivia knew that.

"Sure they are," mumbled her mother as she scrounged around inside the trunk of their car, currently parked on the side of the road. Actually, calling it a car was an insult to vehicles on the road. Try a piece of crap that should have retired a long time ago, sporting rust along the bottom edges of the doors, a muffler that chugged, and a crack across the windshield at just the right height to prove annoying.

Head still tilted, Olivia stared up at the sky, not at all offended by her mother's inattention. Sometimes, not being noticed was the best thing she could hope for. As her mother continued to mumble about the pigsty in the trunk while she tossed things around, Olivia peeked at the unlit road. Nothing distinguished it and Olivia couldn't have said why they halted on this particular stretch. Her mother just suddenly swerved onto the graveled shoulder. Her queries of, "Why are we stopping?" "Are we lost?' and, "Did we run out of gas?" were met with a "because," "no," and "no." She also wanted to ask why they needed to drive almost an hour from the apartment she shared with her aunt, but somehow kind of figured she knew the answer. Just par for the course. In her usual fashion, dear old Mom showed up when she pleased, with a litany of *Sorrys* and a bright smile while she promised to make up for her absence.

Whatever. Olivia knew better than to put any stock in anything Mommy dearest said. Dozens of broken promises later, she knew not to believe anything that came out of her mother's mouth. Still, though, if she played her cards right, she might end up with something – a new sweater, a CD, dinner at McDonald's. Guilt presents, as she liked to call them.

Hopping up onto the hood of the sedan her mother currently drove – a loaner from a *friend,* possibly related to a pig given the condition of the interior – Olivia leaned back and stared at the ring of lights hovering in the sky.

Maybe it's aliens, come to kidnap us. She should be so lucky. It would take a miracle, or her turning sixteen, before she could escape the hellish existence known as her current life. Living with her aunt wasn't too horrible. At least she fed her regular meals, but sharing a room with her two young cousins, cousins she babysat a heck of a lot more than their father did, really wasn't her idea of fun. But it beat sleeping in a car. Her mother's snores were impossible to escape in that case. And the group homes were even worse.

With a triumphant, "Aha!" her mother emerged from the trunk, clasping something baton-shaped. Moments later, an amber-hued flare glowed. A second one lit up in a green burst of light. Waving them around in some weird glow bug dance, her mother pranced in the area beside the car. Strange, yet not the oddest thing she'd seen her mother do. Olivia was used to that kind of erratic behavior from dear old Mom. Actually, the glow stick dance was tame compared to the time her mother staggered home high on something, and drunk to boot. She'd run around the front lawn of the apartment complex trying to catch invisible butterflies, naked, and covered in peanut butter. Child protective services didn't find it as amusing as the neighbors did.

I guess I better hide the car keys again until she sobers up. Olivia sighed. Fooled again. Olivia wondered how she'd missed the signs of inebriation. Usually, she could spot it when her mother had gone on a bender. Then again, despite her funny dance, her mother didn't seem too high, or drunk. No singing or giggling. Weaving or falling. Actually, her mother danced around with a grace Olivia couldn't recall ever seeing. "Whatcha doing?"

"None of your business."

Hmm, possibly sober, but still her ever-delightful self. Snapping her gum, Olivia didn't take offense. Why bother wasting the energy? Back she leaned again, peeking up at the stationary ring of strangeness overhead. As she stared, her breath caught as a single beam of brilliance detached from the larger mass and zipped down toward them. Not just at them, but right overhead, close enough a warm breeze tugged at her loose strands of hair. Holy—word she dared not say aloud lest her aunt guess it and wash her mouth out with soap. Again. Possessed of super-duper auditory powers, Olivia didn't know how her aunt did it, but she always knew when Olivia did or said something bad. And she punished using old school methods. Blech.

With a hum, whatever flew by landed behind some trees. Mommy dearest tossed the glow sticks on to the gravel. Grabbing her purse, she gestured impatiently. "Let's go."

"Go where?"

"Would you stop it with all the questions?" snapped her mother. She grabbed Olivia by the arm and yanked her off the hood. Olivia slid off the metal and her feet hit the ground with a scuff.

Shrugging free of her mother's grip, she frowned. "I'm coming. I was just asking where."

"To see the, um –"

"UFO thingy that landed over in the bushes?"

"Yes. And don't argue."

"Why would I? I want to see what it is too. Maybe it's some super-secret government thing. Or aliens. Aliens would be cool."

"That's just crazy," her mother tittered. "Aliens don't exist. It's probably just a helicopter."

Yeah. Okay. Olivia didn't believe that for a minute and she could tell her mother didn't either, but given she wanted to know what landed, she didn't exactly argue about heading off into a dark patch of forest to encounter who knew what. Couldn't be any worse than the drug addicts and scum that lived in her neighborhood at home. Years later, Olivia still wanted to slap herself for the naivety she'd displayed that night.

Skipping ahead, Olivia made better time than her parent who tottered along in heels not meant for forest treks. A normal child of ten might have feared adventuring in the shadowed woods. Olivia took pride in the fact she was braver and worldlier than other kids her age. Street smart, she called it. The only legacy of her mother she could claim to enjoy.

Smart or not, though, nothing prepared her for the sight that met her eyes when she hit an open patch. As if prepared ahead of time, a clearing existed, one hacked right into the forest, the brush and bramble of it stacked around the outer edges, forcing her to scramble over the impromptu barrier. She could have taken the time to look for a path, but she caught a hint of white. A glow. The mysterious object that flew overhead.

Weather balloon? Moron on a lawn chair flying with helium balloons? The possibilities excited her. While she'd joked about it earlier, though, the last thing she truly expected to see was an honest to goodness spacecraft.

Holy crap. *Sorry, Aunt Ginny.* She ignored the imagined taste of Ivory and took a step, then another toward the sphere hovering a few feet above the ground. Round like a Mentos, but giant-sized, it hummed softly above the ground! Olivia ogled it. Cool. She bent over to look under, but saw nothing to hold it up. The stumps and debris didn't seem to bother it as it bobbed there, a gentle illumination radiating from its shell.

"That is so freakn' cool," she muttered.

"I brought her." Her mother's sudden words startled Olivia. She'd forgotten she wasn't alone. Then the words penetrated. She whirled to look at her mother and didn't see any surprise at all on her face. How did her mother know to expect a UFO? Unless it wasn't an alien craft. Bummer. For a moment, she'd gotten so excited. Olivia peered at it again and let out a squeak as she noted the ramp leading into the probably not-so-candy shell. Standing on the ramp was a hunched, vaguely humanoid creature. Olivia swallowed hard as she stared at the piglike entity, surely a detailed costume, right down to the stench.

"I brought her like you wanted. Now where's my money?"

Olivia whirled. "Your money?" Ten years old or not, she understood the gist of where this was going. "You're selling me? To that?"

"It's for a greater purpose."

"Getting high is not a greater purpose," Olivia sassed, fear sending its tendrils her way.

"I don't have to explain myself to you."

"You will to the cops, though."

"Not if I tell them you ran away."

"But I didn't run away."

"Oh yes, you are. And they'll believe me too."

"But why?" Olivia didn't cry or break down as she asked, but she couldn't help years of curiosity from imbuing her question. "Why do you hate me so much? What have I ever done to you?"

"Exactly." Her mother spat. "What have you done for me, you ungrateful brat? I birth you and what do I get? A few measly extra bucks a month from the government. Not enough for the discomfort I went through carrying you. And your damned father – he promised he'd help. The liar. He couldn't leave town fast enough after you came. It's your fault I'm alone."

Olivia blinked at the tirade, too stunned to feel the pain. It would come later. "So why do you keep coming back?"

"Because you're my kid. I figured maybe one day you'd amount to something. That day is here."

"You can't be serious. You can't sell me. And especially not to that. It's not even human."

"And? He's going to take you to space. Think of it as an adventure."

"No. You can't do this."

"I am."

"You won't get away with this. The cops will figure it out and you'll go to jail."

"The cops won't do shit. I've already gotten away with it twice. Third time's a charm." Her mother's red lips, cracked with dry lipstick, split in a sick smile.

Olivia's mind froze as she thought of the lies her mother told her about Joey, and then Lisa, running away from foster care. Olivia had often wondered if her older siblings found new lives, happier ones that didn't want or need a younger sister messing it up. But no. Her siblings never broke free. Her mother sold them. *Just like she intends to sell me.*

"I'm not going," she stubbornly reiterated. Olivia whirled to run, but something cold blasted her in the back and her limbs literally froze in place. She could only listen and watch as the porky Martian approached, hitching his belt over a hairy belly, his short pants not covering his cloven feet or hairy ankles. Eyeing her in a way that made her skin crawl, the ugly dude paced around Olivia's paralyzed body. "She's a tad young, but she'll do." The creature spat to the side.

"Of course she will. Now pay up or I'm taking her back to her aunt's."

"Do you have any more younglings to sell?"

"Nope. This is the last one. Now fork it over, pigman. I got people to see and things to do." Her mother held out a demanding hand.

"How unfortunate for you that we no longer find you useful. Please enjoy your final payment." Raising a gun, Olivia couldn't even scream when the alien shot her mother, disintegrating her into a pile of dust that blew apart in the light breeze. Then she couldn't care less as Stinky, the name she gave her jailor, carted her into her new home for the next few weeks. Not by any means the worst time of her life, but definitely some of the most frightening, especially since none of the orphans penned together knew what to expect.

She and the other misfits the aliens rounded up coexisted in a kind of weird status, a cross between Peter Pan's lost boys – and girls – and those savage kids on that island with the fly Lord that her aunt made her watch. In some ways, Olivia enjoyed her new life a lot more than her old, especially since she owned one of the top bunks. Life settled into a comfortable routine even if the mush they fed them left a lot to be desired.

And then a second group of pirates attacked their ship. Blood-thirsty bugs, they made no secret of what they wanted humans for – the main ingredient in a supper dish.

Braised Olivia in a sautéed sauce wasn't something she found particularly palatable, so she hid from the new invaders first chance she got, the alien ducts on the ship vast and just the right size for someone petite like herself. She hid so well the pirates vacated the ship with all of her orphan friends and left her alone. All alone. Listing along on a dwindling life support system on a spacecraft stripped of everything they could lay their pinchers on, even at her young age, Olivia knew a death sentence, albeit a slow one, when she saw it.

Then came the morning she awoke, belly taut with hunger, breathing shallow, energy waning, to see a funny-looking guy wearing something out of a history book sitting on the edge of the pallet she'd made for herself. Weak or not, she jumped up brandishing the rusty knife she found during her scavenging. Fear made her young heart pound, but still she bravely faced the smiling guy and in a tremulous voice asked, "Who are you?"

"I am just the greatest of all deities. The be-all and end-all of gods. The one who decides who shall live or –"

A radiant woman stepped up behind him and smacked him in the back of a head. "This is Murphy. And I'm Karma. We *are* gods, but seeing as how the fates say we're to adopt you, you can call us family."

The strangest family the universe probably ever saw, but at the same time, the most loving. The remainder of her childhood passed in a rapid blur as Olivia traveled with her new guardians, learning about whole new cultures and ideas faster than the speed of light – which Karma giggled was such a retro pace.

When her uncle became too stifling and his brand of magic too dangerous, Olivia branched out on her own, hooking up with Ifruum after they met in a jail cell. The rest, as they say, was history.

*

Olivia held her breath as she finished her sad tale. Makl had been silent for a while now. He'd gotten over his raging tantrum when she'd gotten to the part where her mother callously cast her off. For some reason hearing about her mistreatment sent him on a rant where he threatened to kill her until Olivia reminded him her mother was already dead. She found his reaction extreme, but warming at the same time. Despite his oddities, it showed he cared for her on some level.

Not that she did – care, that was. She wasn't stupid. She grasped something was afoot. The super passionate Makl acted like a man on a mission and she had a sneaky suspicion she knew why. Still, when the news arrived via the automated computer announcement that they'd docked at his cousin's planet, she couldn't help a pang of hurt.

He's really going to drop me off.

For some reason, she'd truly expected them to keep on going as they had, pulling off heists, thumbing their nose at authority, getting more and more infamous. She'd even gotten to the point she looked forward to the missions because she couldn't deny she loved the adrenaline of pulling off a well thought out caper and seeing the wild glee in Makl's eyes as they beat the odds. And the sex... Wow.

In her bid to better understand her purple lover, she'd even begun studying the *A Mercenary's Guide to Prosperity* on the side. Some of the rules and sub-clauses sent her into fits of laughter.

Forget living the life of a criminal, though. It seemed her days of being half of the Galactic Lovebirds was over. Makl intended to follow through with his plan to dump her on his cousin as a nanny.

How depressing, but then again, what did she expect him to do? Keep working as a team and screwing like the floppy-eared bunnies on that pink planet several star systems over? So what if they had fun and awesome sex and great talks and...

Oh shit.

To the side she shoved him, hard enough he hit the floor, but not as hard as the realization smacking her between the eyes.

I love purple.

Oh no. When had she allowed that to happen? Why? Had she not learned her lesson growing up? Loving someone, letting herself trust someone, gave them the power to hurt her.

And I am the worst kind of idiot for letting it happen, especially for a cocky, murdering mercenary who never made any bones about the fact he just wanted me for sex.

Thank goodness he reminded her why she didn't want to hook up with him in the first place. Springing from the bed, she dressed quickly and packed even faster. As she nudged Makl aside to grab her favorite bra from the floor to stuff in her luggage, she finally caught his confused gaze. She couldn't hold it, not with the revelation of her love for him still so fresh. Away she looked, searching for something else to pack so she could take a moment to wipe the threatening tears from her eyes.

"What are you doing?" he asked.

"What's it look like I'm doing? Packing, of course. I'm going to need clothes for this nanny gig, aren't I?" She injected an irritable note in her reply.

"Probably a wise thing. Megan would probably kill any female who thought to cavort naked in front of her mate. But, how did you know we'd arrived? Did Ifruum tell you?"

That traitor knew? She'd shave him later in retaliation. "No, he didn't, but it's kind of obvious. We didn't plan a mission or stop, and yet, the ship's landed. You made sure you *cleared your head,*" she air quoted, "a few times more than usual. Add to that woman's intuition and it was a no-brainer."

"You don't seem upset?" Makl said it questioningly as he followed her, her quick strides clacking on the floor.

"Why would I be upset?" She plastered a falsely bright smile on her face. "I did after all promise to do this nanny gig. And as Ifruum reminded me, even thieves need some kind of honor among themselves."

"So you are no longer intending to shirk your promise?"

"Nope." She jabbed at the screen for the docking door, wishing it would damn well hurry up and pressurize before she said something stupid like, "Please let me stay."

"But we were having such fun."

She shrugged. "Yeah. And? Even you should know by now that all good things come to an end.

Best to do it now before you got too clingy. I can't abide a clingy man." She feigned a shudder, but almost lost her stoic look to giggles at the astonishment on his face. "It's been fun, purple. See you around the universe."

As the ship's door opened on to a dusty plain, she blamed the fine particles in the air for the moisture in her eyes. *I am not crying.* Not for him. Not for anyone, not anymore.

As she strode away from the one thing that made her happier than she remembered, the one man who'd made it past the shield she'd erected around her heart, she thanked her lucky stars she did it on her terms before he could truly hurt her.

Now, if only she could find some antacids for the ache in her heart and a tissue for the moisture rolling down her cheeks. Compatible atmosphere her ass. Stupid alien planet, it was already making her sick.

Chapter Fifteen

She's leaving. She's actually leaving me.

Makl watched Olivia walk away, each stride tightening an invisible band around his chest until he thought he'd asphyxiate. A thump on the back had him drawing a heaving breath.

"Well, it was nice knowing you, Makl." Ifruum shambled past, a duffle bag thrown over a hairy shoulder.

"She left." Makl said it softly, disbelieving, unable to hide the unanticipated pain of it.

Ifruum stopped and spun to reply. A shaggy brow rose. "What did you expect? You didn't exactly ask her to stay, did you? This is, after all, what you wanted, why you attempted to abduct her in the first place, and why we're here."

But he never actually expected it to happen. A part of Makl had pictured the scene, a much different scenario. He'd announce they'd arrived at his cousin's planet and tell Olivia it was time to start her new job. She'd cry and beg for him to keep her because he was so magnificent. Being magnanimous, as well as handsome, fearsome, and an excellent lover, he'd let her plead her case – on her knees and back – before begrudgingly giving in after negotiating a daily oral wake up call for the next few planetary cycles. They'd resume their journey, probably dodging missile fire from an irate cousin who still wanted a nanny, and live...well, happily ever after.

None of that happened. Instead, Olivia couldn't escape his presence quick enough. She didn't even give him a last kiss or glance. Not a single tear.

By all the frukxing planets he'd fleeced, it irritated him. Hurt him. Angered him. Crushed him.

Off he stomped back to his ship's main command area, muttering under his breath.

Why can't you admit that you want her?

Because he didn't.

Oh, please, look at the fun you've been having with her.

Pleasure he'd find without her as well, never mind the fact he recalled just how boring his life was before they'd met.

When are you going admit that you love her?

Never. He couldn't. He didn't. He shouldn't. He was a mercenary. Mercenaries didn't love. They killed. They went after priceless things. They got rich and famous. *Until they got mated and settled down.*

Unbidden, Makl recalled a conversation between Tren and his brother before his cousin Jaro hooked up with Aylia. Jaro asked, "What do you mean you've found something more precious than treasure?"

And Tren replied, "If you repeat this, I'll deny it then kill you, but in truth, the greatest treasure of all, the most priceless thing I own, is the love of my mate. Without her, I am nothing. She is the sum of my universe. The reason I plot and kill. She is the most precious thing I can ever hope to possess and the only thing worthy of my life or attention."

Makl, like Jaro at the time, hadn't understood it and thought his cousin a tad touched in the head. It happened to the best of them after a few too many concussions. But now…now Makl had to wonder.

What was fame and fortune if he had no one to share it with? Without Olivia at his side, who would he rehash his greatness with? Who would clap her hands at his wondrous feats? Gasp in horror at his bloodthirsty, murderous side? Moan in pleasure at his excellent prowess as a lover?

Who and what was he without someone to love? No one. *I am alone.* And that just wouldn't do. But he couldn't just turn around and tell her that. A male did not bow to a female, even one he loved. Best he let her play the role of nanny for a little while. Let her miss him and their adventures, then, when he arrived to abduct her, mercenary style – because no way was he asking her permission – she'd be so grateful for his rescue from a life of misery, she'd gladly fall in love with him too.

And if she protested at first, there was always that set of cuffs he'd meant to pull out and try but never got around to. He'd let his excellent skills in the bedroom sway her mind.

A great plan. A perfect plan. A chill went down his back as he could have sworn he heard a ghostly chuckle.

*

Olivia swallowed back the tears as she walked away from Makl toward the unknown. Ifruum, for once, didn't say a word as he scuffed alongside. Uncle Murphy, though, didn't see a need to hold his tongue. He popped into existence beside her, walking stick in one hand, oblivious at the yells from the soldier droids manning the airfield to halt and identify himself.

"What are you doing?" Murphy asked, twirling his baton and somehow blocking the projectiles flying his way.

Halting with her hands held high, Olivia sighed. "What's it look like I'm doing? Trying not to get shot? Or did it not occur to you that suddenly popping into sight on some guy's planet, which is crawling with security, might set off an alarm?"

"Bah. They won't hurt me. I'm a god."

"But I'm not. Remember?"

"Of course I do. I am your uncle." He puffed up his chest indignantly.

"Unfortunately," she mumbled.

"You still haven't answered me. What are you doing? Why are you down here instead of with that purple idiot who has debauched you of any chance at a good marriage?"

"For the millionth time, Uncle Murphy, I never plan on getting married. And for your information, I left because that purple idiot didn't want me."

Her uncle gasped. "Say it isn't so? And here I had the whole marriage planned out. Yards of lace on order and the wedding planners lined up to compete for the chance. Break one of my hundreds of hearts, why don't you," Murphy lamented, hand to his chest.

"I'm sure you'll get over it."

"Of course, I will," Murphy scoffed. "The question is, will you?"

"I don't know what you mean."

"You like the purple mercenary."

Olivia shrugged, unable to stop the fresh wave of hurt at Makl's rejection. "I guess. I mean, it was a fun gig while it lasted." She narrowed her gaze at her uncle. "I don't get why you care. I thought you didn't like him."

"Of course I don't like him. It's my job as guardian to hate all men who come near you. But, as my sister told me when she was chasing me around the sun in the Kippij Galaxy, it's not about what I think that counts, but you. You like him."

"Do not."

"Do too. I'd even go so far as to say you love him."

Olivia grabbed Murphy's necktie and wrapped her fist in it before shaking it. "I do not. Take it back."

"I will not, because it's the truth."

She released him, unable to hold onto her anger, an anger at the veracity of the statement. "Fine. Maybe I do love him. Big whoop-de-do. Lot of good that does me when he obviously doesn't love me back," she yelled, hot tears finally spilling unchecked as she let her anguish emerge in an angry burst. "He didn't want me, just like my mother didn't want me. He just used me until me he didn't need me anymore."

"But I do need you."

The quietly spoken, shocking admission had her spinning on her heel. Makl, his hair standing on end, his pistol smoking, stood there watching with an expression she'd never seen before. He looked desperate. She peered past him and noted the littered droid bodies. He'd battled his way to her side? What for? *And how much did he hear? Oh God, please don't tell me he heard me say I love him.*

"Purple? What are you doing here? I thought you left." She scrubbed at her damp cheeks, trying too late to erase the evidence.

As if he wouldn't notice. His thumb brushed across her damp skin before he cupped her cheek with his large hand. "I meant to. I probably should have. But I can't."

She didn't let herself fall for his obviously feigned chagrin. "Why not? Forget to collect your payment for delivering me?"

"No, I forgot something more important."

"Gas for the spaceship?"

"No."

"Looking for a new sidekick?"

"I already have one."

"That was quick," she muttered, turning around and trying to blink back fresh tears at the callous announcement he'd so quickly replaced her.

"You idiot! And to think they call me the dumb one." Makl yanked her around to face him. He shook her, not too hard, but enough to rattle her teeth. "Don't you see? I didn't realize it until you walked away. I need you."

"To be famous."

"No, I need you because…" Makl clamped his mouth shut, his expression pained. Her spirits sank. He straightened his spine and took a deep breath. "I can't leave because I love you. Are you happy? I set out to abduct a human for my frukxing cousin and instead, I fell in love. With you. The very thought of living without you makes me want to embark upon a murderous rampage. My fame is worthless without you to share it. My life is meaningless if you're not there to lend it color."

"Really?" For a moment, hope lifted her spirits. But… "You say that now, but when the going gets tough, you'll leave me."

"No. I never will. I am not the hag who birthed you. When I give you my word, and you can ask anyone, I keep it. You have nothing to fear from me. I love you, Olivia, even if you are a human barbarian. I will love you until my last breath and I swear before this god as my witness, if anything threatens what we have, I'll kill it."

Her lips twitched. "Your answer to everything is to kill it."

He shrugged. "It's worked for me so far."

"You're asking me to spend my life with a wanted murderer?"

"Hey, I'm willing to spend mine with a thief."

"Acquisition specialist."

"Fancy word for a thief who stole my frukxing heart. Now, are you going to give in gracefully, or am I going to have to torture you? I have cuffs." He raised a hopeful brow.

Hmm, maybe a little torture wouldn't be amiss. Still, though… "A relationship is more than just sex."

Murphy cleared his throat. "If I might interrupt."

"No, you may not!" they both practically shouted.

Makl clasped her hands between his. "It's not just about the sex, even if it is great. I like you. I like talking to you. And sleeping cuddled with you, which I will deny if asked. I like the way you laugh and how your mind works. I even think it's adorable how you still flinch when I kill things. Let me prove how much I love you, that I'm worthy of your trust. Worthy of your love."

Her heart melted, but fear held her back still. "Who says I love you?"

Murphy just couldn't resist butting in again. "You did just a minute ago."

Olivia kicked her uncle in the shin as Ifruum snickered. "Stuff it. Both of you." She focused all her attention on the big purple mercenary in front of her. How could she resist the soft pleading in his eyes? How could she walk away? She knew a proud mercenary like him didn't bare his soul often, if ever. Could she really deny him, deny them both this chance to see if they could make it work? *Can I deny myself a chance at love?*

She couldn't. She wouldn't. She didn't want to spend the rest of her life wondering what could have been. What was one more risk in her life? "You promise to love me forever?"

"Eternally. Please don't leave me. My greatness is nothing without you at my side."

Inhaling a deep breath, the pendulum signaling change hovered invisibly over her head as if the whole universe waited for her answer. "I love you, purple."

Makl whooped and swung her in his arms, whirling her about in a dizzying arc. He swooped in for a kiss. It might have turned into something more, but as usual, Fate – the cousin Murphy refused to talk to – intervened.

A voice boomed across the plains, amplified by hidden speakers. "If you're done with your frukxing love fest, would you mind getting your buttocks to the house now? My son has just woken up and is screaming. Again. Don't make me come and get you." The low growled threat would have proven more effective without the shrill wail of a baby.

Makl wrapped his fingers around hers in a tight grip. "Only for you would I face my cousin and his spawn. Remember that at my funeral."

Together, they made their way to the compound housing a mansion the size Olivia never imagined, but immediately coveted. "We could make a fortune here," she muttered to Makl.

"I know, but first we'd have to get through my family and trust me, they're not people you want to provoke."

Once Olivia met the formidable cousin, Tren – a scary-looking purple dude with bloodshot eyes and hair standing on end – she could see why. The fact Tren's wife was human took Olivia by surprise. Somehow, in all their discussions, Makl forgot to mention the fact his cousins married humans. But who had time to converse when the yelling started and people scattered?

A bundle of red-faced rage was thrust at her and people retreated so quickly Olivia wondered if they'd set new fast walking records. Abandoned, except for Makl, who unabashedly held his hands over his ears, Olivia held the screaming baby out at arm's-length.

Face screwed up and beet red, the tyke yelled his little brains out, his clenched fists waving. Oh, this wouldn't do at all. Olivia marched after his fleeing parents, following the sounds of shouting –

which she could hear over the hiccups of the calming child. She found Tren and Megan downstairs facing off. However, whatever argument they had stopped before she entered the room. Junior started bellowing again in the silence.

Face pained, Tren barked, albeit in a hushed tone, "Why is the baby still crying?"

"Because I am not its mommy or daddy." Olivia stated waving the noisemaker at them.

"Shhh. Don't do that." Megan's eyes widened. "He's fragile. Have you seen the size of him? He could break if you shake him too hard."

"He's a baby, not a piece of porcelain," Olivia snorted, waggling him again. To everyone's surprise, the screaming stopped. All eyes went to the child and Olivia froze mid-motion. The screaming started again. Olivia jiggled him lightly. No change. Harder. The child shut his mouth and stared at her.

"See? The human nanny I found you is working already," Tren announced triumphantly to his wife.

"Okay, it's a start, but does this mean we're going to have to shake the baby constantly?" Megan frowned. "I could have sworn that wasn't good for them."

"Because it's not," Olivia practically shouted. "Did neither of you read a book about babies at all before having one?"

"Of course not." Tren straightened his shoulders as he replied indignantly. "Child rearing is a woman's job. I step in when it is time to discipline and begin training."

"Woman's job?" Megan's spine went ramrod straight. "Is this your way of implying I didn't do my job?"

Back and forth the yelling went; the baby with his thumb tucked in his mouth watched contentedly. Not that Olivia initially noticed, but when she did, she drew their attention to it. "Um, guys. How often do you argue in front of the baby?"

Interrupted, they halted, Megan biting her lip in obvious chagrin at having lost control in front of her child. The baby's face screwed up. Olivia gave him a little shake with a don't-you-dare look. He stopped.

"We don't argue in front of the kid. Even I know that's not healthy." Megan rolled her eyes.

"We don't allow loud noises of any kind lest they disturb my son."

Olivia tsked. "And that's your problem. I'll bet you guys argued the entire pregnancy."

"Maybe," Megan said, hedging.

"All the time," Tren unabashedly admitted. "It's great foreplay."

Megan slapped him in the arm, not that her husband noticed.

"And when the baby was born?" Olivia questioned.

"We stopped so he could sleep."

"So you shoved the baby into the world from his nice warm spot and took away the one thing he probably remembered, the two of you shouting. And, um, wrestling, which probably shook him around quite a bit."

They nodded.

Olivia sighed. "Idiots. He's used to the commotion. Without it, he feels lost." Her words were met with a heavy quiet as Tren and his wife looked at each other. Then the baby let out a loud yell to remind them he was there.

Megan grabbed her son from Olivia as his lower lip trembled. The mother shook him. He perked up. She bounced him again. A smile cracked his lips. Megan gasped and dropped him.

Tren dove and hit the ground, catching the falling baby who let out a giggle. Stunned silence froze everyone. All eyes went to the baby. He fidgeted under all the gazes, then let out a mighty shriek.

Tren tossed the baby up. Megan gasped. Tren caught him. Giggle. Pout. Toss. Smile. Olivia didn't know how long the two parents, stupid grins on their faces, played catch the falling baby, a game Olivia felt sure would end in a head bashing. But, the father never missed a catch and played with his son long enough that at one point Olivia loudly reminded them when the crying resumed that the child probably needed a feeding and a nap.

Actually, everyone had a nap. Hers involved little shut eye, but featured a bed with a naked mercenary in it.

It still blew her mind that he'd come back for her, and within minutes of her leaving. It stunned her even more that he claimed to care for her. *He loves me.*

She straddled her purple mercenary and pulled on his nipple ring. "Say it again."

"Say what? Suck me harder? Can't I get a moment to recover, you insatiable barbarian?"

Olivia laughed. "No, purple. The other thing."

A smile softened his lips. "You mean that I love you? I do. I didn't realize it until you walked away, but I do with all of my mighty being. But don't think this means you'll get whatever you want. I'm still in charge."

She wiggled atop him. "Are you so sure about that?"

Rolled under him quick as a blink, he spent the next little while arguing with her about who wore the pants in their relationship, until she pointed out that in the bedroom, neither of them wore anything, which then started a discussion on whether women should be allowed to wear pants or not, which led to a new argument. And well, as they say, the rest is history, but at least her story now involved a happily ever after.

And a fabulous new nickname. Beloved. But that one wasn't for the cameras, even if news of their actual nuptials made the news, courtesy of Makl's marketing manager.

The Galactic Lovebirds tie the knot. Does this mean their crime spree days are over?

Pfft. As if.

Epilogue

Makl whistled as he bided his time. The alien sporting a dark cowl hovering over him didn't appreciate it one bit.

"Would you stop acting so cheerful? It's unseemly, given you're about to die."

"No I'm not."

The executioner hefted his weapon. "My axe says you are."

"But the love my mate bears for me says otherwise," Makl bragged as Olivia rushed into the room with not a moment to spare. She swung a priceless vase – No! – and clobbered the nearest guard on the head, shattering the fragile pottery, knocking her target out. Frukxing human morals still wouldn't let her kill with impunity. Yet, she loved him – yes, she loved him – enough that she came to his rescue, screaming something that he could have sworn was, "Freedom!" which made no real sense, but always seemed to put a savage grin on her face.

Whatever she yelled, she distracted his executioner long enough that she managed to shoot the hooded alien in the shoulder. Despite it not being a deadly strike, it did the trick. The axe dropped. Makl rolled onto it and neatly sliced the bonds around his wrists, losing only a bit of blood in the process. Taking possession of the blunt weapon, after a brief struggle he of course won, he made short work of the executioner's head then attacked the ropes binding his ankles. Freed, he sprang to his feet.

"You came back for me," he exclaimed. "I knew you cared."

She wrinkled her nose. "Ugh. Don't make me regret it already, okay? Come on. Let's blow this joint before we actually have to fight our way out."

A handful of guards came running into the room.

"Oops, too late."

Rolling her eyes, Olivia leaned against a wall and waited while Makl increased his kill count. He'd slowed down the murdering and assassinations a lot since he discovered he loved his human and couldn't live without her. For some reason, having more deaths under his belt than his cousin didn't seem as important anymore. Actually, all the prizes and bounties in the universe paled in comparison to the treasure he'd found. Love.

But being in love didn't mean he'd retired. The Galactic Lovebirds were still going strong, leaving a trail of robberies and videos of their passion wherever they went. And soon, if the bribe he'd left with the goddess of fertility in the Venusian star system proved fruitful, he'd have a little mercenary to follow in their footsteps. A son he could hand his battered copy of *A Mercenary's Guide to Prosperity* to.

Or maybe he'd have a daughter who would need a father's deadly skills to keep her safe from mercenaries like him. Because he just knew any daughter of his would be beautiful, brave, and wonderful, just like the mate he'd found. After all, he worshipped Karma, and he knew better than to think his years of debauchery wouldn't come back to haunt. However, with his beloved barbarian at his side supporting him, he looked forward to the challenge, and the future.

*

Murphy sighed as he leaned back in his cosmic lazy chair, feet up watching the unfolding scene. He already missed his adventures with his niece Olivia, but at least he'd left her in the capable – if cocky – hands of a warrior who would cherish her. He just couldn't believe how long it took the purple idiot to come to his senses. Had he skipped the chapter on finding his one true mate?

"He didn't skip it because he never had it," Karma announced, reading his thoughts as she popped into existence alongside him, dressed in an eye popping ensemble that involved a lot of pink and black feathers.

"How could he not have it? It's part of every handbook."

Reaching into a pocket – which by all rights shouldn't exist in her skimpy garment – Karma pulled out a sheaf of paper and brandished it with a smirk. "Not his handbook. I pulled this section out a while back."

"Because?"

"Because he doubted my existence." Her lower lip jutted.

"But isn't he one of your followers now?"

"Now he is. But he wasn't when I did it."

"And did you never think to put it back or at least tell him? It would have made my job getting our niece settled down a lot easier."

"I could have. However…" His sister winked. "Everyone knows Karma's a bitch."

*

Part of the missing chapter from Makl's mercenary handbook.

In summary, when you find your one true mate, there are really only a few options you can choose.

Kill her before you get emotionally invested. A coward's route, but effective for the warrior who is adamant about remaining unfettered and wishes to live alone.

Run – as far and fast as you can until you've sown all your seeds of destruction, killed to your heart's content, and plowed as many fertile fields as you can. Then, find the female, grant her a divorce from a mate if she has one – we recommend a permanent, deadly one – and settle down to start your own line of mercenaries.

But our recommendation is marry her. And don't *just* marry her, but love her with everything you have because you really only get one chance at happiness. One shot at true love, and for a mercenary, there is nothing more precious, more valuable, nothing more worth protecting than the bond you can share with the right female.

And remember, if anything threatens your love, don't hesitate. Kill it. It is after all the mercenary way.

The End

Printed in Great Britain
by Amazon